THE HEADMASTER

By ANDY RUSSO

COPYRIGHT © ANDY PARKER 2024

ALL RIGHTS RESERVED.

No part of this book may be reproduced or transmitted in any form by any means, electronic or mechanical, including photocopying and recording, or by any information storage and retrieval system, except as may be expressly permitted in writing from the author.

ISBN: 9798301399633

ABOUT THE AUTHOR

My name is Andy Parker, born August 1966 in Teddington. In 1985 I had a serious car crash which put me in a wheelchair for the rest of my life. But I have a strong disposition and with strong support of friends and family I've always accomplished things I wanted to do and this novel is no exception. I've always had a love of thrillers and crime novels, from a young age being fascinated by Agatha Christie and Alfred Hitchcock and then turning my attention to my favourite authors John Grisham and Michael Connelly. This is my first book under pen name Andy Russo, there are plenty more in the pipeline, all authors have to start somewhere so my next goal is to become a best-selling author!

PROLOGUE

The Louisiana swamp stretched out in every direction, a tangled, oppressive mass of green. It was the kind of place that seemed to breathe on its own, pulsing with life beneath the stillness. The early morning mist clung to the cypress trees, wrapping their gnarled trunks in a ghostly shroud. Every now and then, a ripple broke the surface of the black water, sending concentric circles outward before they were swallowed again by the swamp.

Beneath the dense canopy, the world was a muted twilight, and the air was thick with the scent of decay and earth. The swamp was a place of secrets, where the line between the living and the dead blurred like the mist that curled around the cypress knees. It was a place that invited stories—stories of lost souls, cursed waters, and creatures that didn't belong to the world of men. And as the sun fought to break through the mist, it cast long, twisted shadows that made the swamp appear even more alive, as if it was watching, waiting.

The fisherman had been out on the water since before dawn, his small boat barely disturbing the still surface as he navigated the narrow channels. He had grown up in these parts, and knew every twist and turn of the swamp like the back of his hand. But no matter how familiar he was with it, there was always a part of him that stayed on edge, a whisper in the back of his mind that reminded him the swamp was not a place to be taken lightly.

He was heading toward a favourite fishing spot, where the water was deep and the fish plentiful. But as he rounded a bend, something caught his eye—a shape floating just beneath the surface, bobbing gently with the current. At first, he thought it might be a log or a piece of driftwood. But as he drew closer, his breath caught in his throat.

It was a body.

The fisherman hesitated, his hand tightening on the oar as he debated what to do. He had found bodies in the swamp before—people who had wandered in and never come out, victims of the swamp's many dangers. Most were tourists, city folk who didn't understand the risks. But there was something different about this one, something that made his skin crawl.

He leaned over the side of the boat, using the oar to nudge the body closer. The water was dark and murky, hiding the full extent of the damage. But as the body turned, the fisherman's heart slammed against his ribs.

The man's torso was grotesquely mangled, torn apart by powerful jaws. The flesh was ragged, chunks missing where the gator had feasted. The sight was grisly, but not unfamiliar. The swamp was home to more alligators than people, and they were ruthless when it came to feeding. But it wasn't the gator's handiwork that made the fisherman's blood run cold.

The body was missing its head.

Where the neck should have been was a stump, the flesh and bone clean and even. The fisherman recoiled, bile rising in his throat. An alligator could have done this, he told himself. They were known to bite clean through a limb, even a head, if they caught their prey just right. But deep down, he knew this wasn't the work of a gator.

The body had been torn open by the gator, no doubt about that. But something, or someone, had taken the man's head.

Horror settled in the fisherman's chest, a heavy weight that made it hard to breathe. He knew he should leave, get back to town, and tell the authorities. But the swamp had other ideas. The water around the boat rippled, and for a moment, he thought he saw something moving beneath the surface, something large and serpentine. His heart pounded in his ears as he scanned the water, but whatever it was, it was gone.

He forced himself to look at the body again, at the gaping wound where the head should have been. This wasn't an accident. This was something else, something worse. The swamp had claimed many lives over the years, but this was different. This was deliberate.

The fisherman backed away from the edge of the boat, his hands shaking as he fumbled with the oar. He needed to get out of here, away from this place, away from whatever had done this. He could feel the swamp closing in around him, the trees leaning in as if they were watching, waiting to see what he would do.

As he turned the boat around, the mist thickened, swallowing the body as it drifted back into the darkness. The fisherman didn't look back. He didn't need to. The image of the mangled torso, of the missing head, was burned into his mind.

The swamp was a place of secrets, and today, he had stumbled onto one he wished he hadn't.

CHAPTER ONE

Sheriff James Landry had seen a lot in his years patrolling the bayou. He'd been born and raised in the swamp, a grizzled veteran of its tangled depths and murky waters. The swamp was in his blood, and there wasn't much that could rattle him. But as he stood on the banks of that narrow channel, staring down at the mangled body sprawled on the ground, he felt a cold knot of unease twist in his gut.

The fisherman who had discovered the body stood a few paces back, pale and trembling as he recounted what he'd seen. Landry listened with half an ear, and his attention focused on the corpse before him. The body was a mess of torn flesh and broken bones, a sight all too familiar to the sheriff. But there was something off about this one, something that set his nerves on edge.

The head was gone, severed clean from the neck, and the torso had been ravaged by what was unmistakably a gator. That much was clear. But Landry's eyes were drawn to the stump where the head should have been. He crouched down beside the body, examining the wound with a practised eye.

It wasn't the jagged tear of an animal's bite. No, this was something different, something deliberate. The cut was clean and precise—a straight line through muscle and bone. Landry narrowed his eyes, reaching out to gently lift the edge of the torn flesh. The more he looked, the more certain he became. This wasn't the work of a gator.

"Get him back," Landry said, his voice a low growl as he straightened up. "Get him fingerprinted. See if he's in the database."

One of the deputies, a young kid fresh out of the academy, looked up from where he'd been taking notes. "You think he's local, Sheriff?"

"If he is, he'll be in the system," Landry replied, his tone curt. "If he's not, we've got bigger problems."

The deputy nodded and hurried off to relay the orders. Landry watched him go, then turned his attention back to the body. He'd seen his share of gator attacks, and they were always brutal, messy affairs. But this... this was different. The precision of the dismemberment was chilling, like someone had taken their time, ensuring the cut was perfect. It reminded him more of a butcher at work, or a swordsman—someone who knew exactly what they were doing.

He scanned the area, taking in the thick tangle of cypress trees, the sluggish water, and the thick mist that still clung to the swamp like a shroud. The place felt different today, heavier somehow, as if the swamp itself was holding its breath.

Landry had always respected the swamp, and knew that it was a living thing with its own rules and secrets. But he'd never felt fear out here, not like this. Whoever—or whatever—had done this wasn't just some random predator. This was calculated, methodically, and that's what bothered him the most. The bayou had its share of dangers, but this was something else entirely.

He bent down again, inspecting the wound one last time before rising to his feet. He couldn't shake the feeling that he was missing something, that there was a piece of this puzzle he hadn't yet seen. The gator had ripped the body apart; that much was clear. But the head… it was as if it had been taken, almost like a trophy.

"Sheriff," the young deputy called out as he returned, looking a little pale himself. "We've got the body loaded up. I'll head back to the station, get those prints run."

Landry nodded, his mind still on the body. "Good. Make it quick. And check with the coroner—see if he's ever seen anything like this before."

The deputy hesitated, then asked, "You think this could be connected to something… bigger?"

Landry didn't answer right away. He kept his eyes on the water, watching as the last ripples from the boat slowly faded away. "I don't know," he said finally, his voice grim. "But whatever it is, it's not just the gators we need to worry about."

The young deputy swallowed hard and nodded before heading off to the station. Landry stayed behind for a moment longer, taking in the scene one last time. The swamp was quiet now, the mist beginning to lift as the sun climbed higher in the sky. But the sheriff knew better than to be fooled by the calm. The swamp might look peaceful on the surface, but beneath that still water, there were things that waited, hidden from sight.

Landry ran a hand over his stubbled jaw, then turned and made his way back to his truck. There was work to be done, questions to be answered……..

CHAPTER TWO

The ride back to Houma was tense and silent, the young deputy's mind racing as he glanced in the rearview mirror at the black body bag secured in the back of the van. The swamp had a way of getting under your skin, and what he'd seen that morning had shaken him more than he cared to admit. He tried to focus on the road, but the image of the mutilated body kept flashing in his mind—a grim reminder that the swamp wasn't the only thing out there to fear.

By the time he pulled into the small parking lot behind the Houma County Sheriff's Office, the sun was well above the horizon, but it did little to dispel the chill that had settled in his bones. The pathologist was already waiting for him, a middle-aged man with grey hair and a calm demeanour that came from years of dealing with the aftermath of violence. Dr. Henry Broussard had seen it all, or so he liked to think. But as the deputy helped him wheel the body into the morgue, even Broussard couldn't suppress a grimace.

"Gator?" the pathologist asked, already knowing the answer.

"Mostly," the deputy replied, his voice tight. "But there's more to it. Sheriff Landry thinks it might be something else—something deliberate."

Broussard raised an eyebrow but said nothing as he unzipped the bag. The stench hit them both immediately, a foul mix of swamp water and decomposing flesh. The pathologist worked quickly, pulling on gloves and setting up his tools. As he began his examination, the deputy took a step back, trying to put some distance between himself and the gruesome sight.

It didn't take long for Broussard to confirm what Landry had suspected. The torso, legs, and arms were all marred with jagged gashes and torn flesh—unmistakable signs of an alligator attack. But the neck wound was different. Broussard frowned as he examined the cut, running a gloved finger along the edge of the severed neck.

"This wasn't done by an animal," Broussard said, his voice matter-of-fact. "This was a clean cut. One swipe, straight through the bone. Whoever did this knew what they were doing."

The deputy swallowed hard. "You mean like a sword?"

"Something like that," Broussard replied. "A machete could do it, but not this cleanly. My guess is a sword or a very sharp blade. Either way, it was deliberate."

The deputy felt a shiver run down his spine. The idea of someone out there wielding a sword in the bayou, decapitating people, was too surreal to process. But then again, so was everything about this case.

"Let's get his fingerprints," the deputy said, trying to focus on the task at hand.

Broussard nodded and quickly went to work. The process was straightforward, but the tension in the room was palpable. When the prints were finally taken, the deputy headed to the office to run them through the database. He tapped his foot impatiently as the system processed the information, the seconds stretching into what felt like hours. Finally, the screen blinked, and a match appeared.

"John Jacobs," the deputy read aloud. "Fifty-five years old. Known around here as John Boy."

Broussard looked up from his work, recognition flickering in his eyes. "John Boy? The one who ran that fishing charter out of Terrebonne Parish?"

"Yeah," the deputy replied, scanning through the rest of the file. "Looks like his business had been going downhill for a while. And… here we go. He was just released a few weeks ago. Found not guilty in a molestation case—young girls."

The room went quiet, the weight of the revelation settling over them both. John Boy wasn't exactly a popular figure in Houma, especially after the trial. There had been whispers, and rumours that the only reason he got off was a lack of evidence, but everyone knew there was more to it. The thought of his violent end didn't bring much sympathy.

Sheriff Landry arrived at the station not long after, his heavy boots echoing through the narrow halls as he made his way straight to the autopsy room. The scent of antiseptic hit him as he pushed open the door, finding Dr. Broussard hunched over the examination table, his expression grim. The young deputy, pale and tight-lipped, stood nearby, his eyes flicking nervously between the body and the sheriff. Broussard didn't waste time, quickly detailing the results—the gator bites were vicious but secondary, the decapitation a clean, deliberate cut. Landry's jaw tightened as the deputy filled him in on the identity of the victim: John Boy Jacobs, a name still fresh in everyone's mind after his recent acquittal on child molestation charges. The room seemed to grow colder as the weight of the situation settled over them all.

"He's got a younger brother," the deputy continued. "Daryl Jacobs. Runs a swamp tour operation not far from John Boy's place."

Landry nodded, his expression neutral. "We'd better take a spin over there. Give him the news."

As he left the morgue, the weight of the situation settled on Landry like the humid air outside. The swamp had claimed another life, but this time, it wasn't just nature at work. There was something darker at play, something that went beyond the dangers of the bayou. And as he climbed into his Deputy's car and headed toward Daryl Jacobs's place, he couldn't shake the feeling that this was just the beginning.

CHAPTER THREE

Sheriff Landry's cruiser rumbled down the narrow dirt road, the sound of gravel crunching beneath the tyres blending with the hum of cicadas in the thick Louisiana air. Beside him, the young deputy fidgeted nervously, still shaken from the morning's events. Landry, ever the steady presence, kept his eyes forward, the familiar landscape of the bayou rolling by like an old film he'd seen a thousand times.

They arrived at Daryl's Swamp Tours; a sprawling wooden shack perched precariously on the edge of the swamp. The place was a mishmash of weathered boards, faded signs, and old fishing gear, all of it looking like it had been there for decades. A handful of tourists milled about the property, flipping through brochures and checking the tour times posted on a creaky bulletin board. The smell of swamp water and diesel fuel hung heavy in the air, mingling with the scent of the cypress trees that lined the riverbank.

As Landry and his deputy stepped out of the car, a young woman bounded out of the office with a wide smile. She was striking—buxom, with long blonde hair that fell in waves over her shoulders, and a tattoo of a serpent that coiled down one arm. She moved with a confident, almost playful energy, and her smile widened as she approached them.

"What can I do for you, Sheriff?" she asked, her voice a sultry drawl that matched her appearance.

The young deputy's face flushed a deep red as he struggled to find his voice, taken aback by her presence. Landry chuckled, giving him a knowing look before turning back to the woman.

"We need to speak to your boss," Landry said, his tone friendly but firm.

"Daryl's just coming in now," she replied, gesturing toward the river where a flat-bottomed boat was gliding toward the dock. "Shouldn't be long."

Landry nodded, watching as the boat pulled up to the dock. The tourists onboard, a mix of curious visitors and adventurous souls, began to disembark, chattering excitedly about the sights they'd seen. The tour guide, a burly man in his forties with a thick beard and sun-weathered skin, helped them off the boat with practised ease. This was Daryl Jacobs, the younger brother of John Boy.

Landry and his deputy waited until the last of the tourists had wandered off toward the parking lot, then made their way down to the dock. Daryl looked up as they approached, his expression hardening when he recognized the sheriff.

"Sheriff Landry," Daryl greeted, his voice a gravelly rumble as he secured the boat. "What brings you out here?"

"Need to talk to you, Daryl," Landry said, his voice low. "It's about John Boy."

Daryl's eyes narrowed, and he wiped his hands on a dirty rag before crossing his arms over his chest. "What about him?"

Landry hesitated for a moment, then decided there was no point in sugarcoating it. "He's dead, Daryl. We found his body this morning in the swamp."

The air seemed to go still, the sounds of the bayou fading into the background as Daryl processed the news. His face twisted with anger, his hands clenching into fists. "Dead? How?"

Landry exchanged a glance with his deputy before answering. "Gator got him, but there's more to it than that. Someone took his head, Daryl. It wasn't just the gator."

Daryl's eyes darkened, a mix of grief and fury flashing across his face. "One of those parents," he spat, his voice thick with rage. "It's gotta be one of those damn parents from the trial. They couldn't let it go, couldn't accept that John Boy was innocent."

The young deputy shifted uncomfortably, his eyes darting between Daryl and Landry. The sheriff remained calm, meeting Daryl's gaze with a steady intensity. "We don't know that yet, Daryl. But we're going to find out who did this. I need you to stay calm and let us handle it."

Daryl's jaw tightened, his body trembling with barely restrained anger. "Calm? You Do you want me to stay calm while some bastard out there thinks they can get away with this? John Boy wasn't perfect, but he didn't deserve this. If you don't find out, who did it, I will. And I won't be nearly as nice about it."

Landry nodded, understanding the depth of Daryl's pain, but knowing that letting him go off on his own would only lead to more bloodshed. "I get it, Daryl. I do. But you must let us do our job. We're going to find out who did this, and they'll pay for it, one way or another."

Daryl glared at him for a long moment, then finally looked away, his fists slowly unclenching. "You better," he muttered, turning back to the boat. "Because if you don't, there won't be anything left of them when I'm done."

Landry watched him for a moment, then gave the deputy a nod, signalling it was time to go. As they walked back to the car, the young deputy glanced nervously over his shoulder at Daryl, who was already busying himself with the boat, though the tension in his shoulders was impossible to miss.

"Think he'll go after them, Sheriff?" the deputy asked quietly as they climbed into the cruiser.

"If we don't find who did this quick, he just might," Landry replied, starting the engine. "And that's something we can't afford to let happen."

The cruiser pulled away from the dock, leaving the swamp and Daryl's smouldering anger behind. But as they drove back toward Houma, Landry couldn't shake the feeling that this was only the beginning of a storm that had been brewing for a long time. The swamp had secrets, and they were starting to surface, one bloody piece at a time.

CHAPTER FOUR

Sheriff Landry sat at his worn wooden desk, the hum of the overhead fan barely masking the tension that hung in the room. The John Jacobs trial had ended in a controversial acquittal, but Landry's work was far from done. His focus was now on understanding why Jacobs had targeted these specific girls. He began by scrutinizing the background of Olivia Sims, a thirteen-year-old Black girl whose testimony had been both heartbreaking and infuriating. Jacobs had picked her up from school, pretending to know her mother, and had used that false familiarity to get her into his truck. Olivia's father was absent, leaving her to be raised by her hardworking, single mother, Cassandra Sims, who struggled to make ends meet. As Landry delved into Olivia's family dynamics, he couldn't shake the feeling that Jacobs had preyed on the vulnerability inherent in Olivia's situation—a young girl with only her overburdened mother to protect her.

Charlotte Franklin was another young black girl at ten years old the youngest. Jacobs had enticed her with sweets into a male restroom, but fortunately, the encounter had been interrupted before it escalated. Someone had walked into the restroom, startling Jacobs, who quickly told Charlotte to scram. She had bolted out of the restroom, frightened and confused, but safe. Charlotte's grandparents, both in their seventies, had raised her after her parents had died in a car accident. They were loving but frail, struggling with the energy and awareness needed to protect a child from a predator like Jacobs. Sheriff Landry couldn't help but feel a deep sense of sorrow for Charlotte's situation. Her vulnerability had been obvious evident to Jacobs, who had targeted her precisely because she was under the care of guardians who were not equipped to shield her from such dangers.

 Finally, there was Emma Knight, the third and oldest victim. At fifteen, Emma was a white girl from a seemingly stable household. But as Landry delved deeper, more profoundly, he uncovered cracks in the family's facade. Emma's father, Mr. Knight, was a stern man with a reputation for being overly protective of his daughter. The incident with Jacobs had taken place in Emma's own bedroom—a space that should have been her sanctuary. According to Mr. Knight's testimony, he had caught Jacobs in Emma's room late one night. The intruder claimed that he had been invited there by Emma herself, using crude language that had sent Mr. Knight into a blind rage. Jacobs was lucky to have escaped with just a few bruises after Mr. Knight had physically thrown him out of the house. Emma vehemently denied ever inviting Jacobs, insisting that she had no idea how he had entered her room.

Landry spent several hours piecing together the details of each case. The more he thought about it, the more he realized realised that the parentage and guardianship of these girls played a crucial role in Jacobs' choice of victims. Olivia, with only her overworked mother to protect her, had been an easy target. Charlotte, living with elderly grandparents who couldn't keep a close eye on her, had been another. But Emma's case was different. Her father was not only present but fiercely protective—almost too protective.

It was Mr. Knight who stood out in Landry's mind. Of all the victims' families, he was the only one who seemed truly capable of taking matters into his own hands. The man's anger was palpable, and his threats against Jacobs had been explicit. "Ever go near my daughter again, and you're a dead man," Mr. Knight had shouted as he threw Jacobs out of his house. Landry couldn't shake the feeling that Mr. Knight might have been pushed beyond the breaking point.

As the sheriff reviewed the evidence again, he found himself drawn to one unsettling conclusion: Mr. Knight was the only person in the entire case who had the motive, the means, and the opportunity to ensure that John Jacobs never harmed another girl again.

Sheriff Landry knew he had to tread carefully. Jacobs was on trial, but the trial was not for murder—yet. But if something were to happen to Jacobs, all eyes would turn to Mr. Knight, and Landry would have to be the one to bring him in. He wasn't sure how he felt about that, but he knew what his duty required.

As the sun began to rise, casting a pale light over the sleepy town, Landry made a silent vow. He would get to the bottom of this, no matter where the evidence led. Whether Mr. Knight was a desperate father pushed too far or a man capable of cold-blooded murder, Landry would uncover the truth.

CHAPTER FIVE

Sheriff Landry jumped into his cruiser, the sun just setting on the horizon, casting long shadows over the small town. The air was still and warm, the remnants of a summer day clinging to the evening like a heavy blanket. Landry knew he had a job to do, and tonight, that job led him to the grand estate of Mr. Knight. The Knight family had money, a lot of it, and their mansion sat atop a hill, overlooking the rest of the town like a king's castle. In the dimming light, it was almost intimidating, a fortress where secrets could easily quickly be buried.

John Boy Jacobs had been a name whispered in disgust, especially after what had happened in that trial. The town had been divided, but the jury had spoken, and Jacobs had walked away a free man, much to the fury of many, especially Mr. Knight. Of the three families who could have taken justice into their own hands, it was only Mr. Knight who had both the means and the raw anger to do something as drastic as murder.

Landry's tyres crunched on the gravel driveway as he pulled up to the Knight residence. The house loomed over him, a towering structure of brick and stone, its windows dark except for a faint light in what he knew was the study. The sheriff cut the engine and sat for a moment, letting the silence of the evening settle around him. There was a stillness here, a sense that something was just out of place, waiting to be uncovered.

He approached the front door, his boots echoing on the stone steps. Before he could knock, the door swung open, revealing Mr. Knight standing there, as if he had been expecting the visit. Landry took in the man before him—a tall, broad-shouldered figure, with a face that had aged too quickly from the stress of the past months. His eyes were sharp, but there was something else there, too, something that Landry couldn't quite place.

"Evening, Sheriff," Mr. Knight greeted him, his voice calm, controlled.

"Evening, Mr. Knight. Mind if I come in?" Landry asked, though it was more a statement than a question.

Mr. Knight stepped aside, allowing the sheriff to enter. The house was as grand inside as it was outside, with high ceilings and expensive furnishings. But it felt cold, too. The warmth of family seemed to have been drained from it, leaving only the shell of wealth and status.

Landry followed Mr. Knight into the study, where Mrs. Knight was already seated on a plush armchair, her hands clasped tightly in her lap. She offered a polite smile, but her eyes were wary, nervous. Landry nodded to her before taking a seat opposite the pair.

"I'm sure you know why I'm here," Landry began, leaning forward slightly.

Mr. Knight nodded. "I assume it's about John Boy Jacobs."

"That's right. You know he was found dead last night."

"I heard," Mr. Knight said, his tone measured. "But you don't think I had anything to do with that, do you, Sheriff?"

Landry studied him, trying to read between the lines of the man's calm demeanour. "I know you were angry, Mr. Knight. Anyone would have been, especially after finding Jacobs in your daughter's bedroom. But that kind of anger can drive a man to do things he wouldn't normally consider."

Mr. Knight stiffened, his jaw clenching slightly. "I won't deny that I was furious, Sheriff. When I found that man in my daughter Emma's bedroom, I... I lost control. Any father would. But I would never kill another human being. I'm a Christian, Sheriff. I believe in justice, but not that kind of justice."

"You say that, but sometimes belief isn't enough to hold back what a person's feeling," Landry countered. "And I have to ask—where were you last night?"

"I was at home, here, with my wife," Mr. Knight replied, his voice steady. "We were together all evening, weren't we, dear?"

Mrs. Knight nodded quickly, her eyes flitting between her husband and the sheriff. "Yes, Sheriff. We were both here. We had dinner, and then we stayed in for the night. Neither of us left the house."

Landry glanced between them; the alibi was solid, and Landry, deep down did believe them. Even though Landry had a temper and maybe there was something not quite right in the atmosphere, he didn't believe Mr. Knight was a killer.

"I see," Landry said finally, leaning back in his chair. "Well, I had to ask. I'm sure you understand."

"Of course," Mr. Knight replied, his tone still polite but with an edge of finality. "But I assure you, Sheriff, I had nothing to do with Jacobs' death. I may have been angry, disgusted even, with the outcome of that trial, but I was here, with my wife, the entire night."

Landry nodded, though he didn't feel any closer to the truth. "Thank you for your time, Mr. Knight. Mrs. Knight," he added, tipping his hat slightly to her as he rose to leave.

As he made his way back to his car, the night fully settled in around him, ; Landry couldn't shake the feeling that something wasn't adding up. Mr. Knight had the motive, the means, and the opportunity, but the man he had just spoken to seemed far too controlled, far too collected for someone who might have just committed murder. But then again, grief and anger could manifest in strange ways.

The sheriff climbed back into his car; , the leather seat warm from the day's heat. He sat there for a moment, staring back at the house, its windows now completely dark. There was something there, ; he could feel it, but it was just out of reach. He would have to dig deeper, find that one loose thread that could unravel everything.

As Landry started the engine and pulled away, his mind was already racing ahead, thinking of his next move. The town was small, and secrets had a way of surfacing when you least expected them. He just had to be patient, and vigilant. The truth would come to light— eventually. But first he had to go back to Daryll Jacobs and assure him none of the families had taken the matter into their own hands.

CHAPTER SIX

A storm was brewing on the horizon, the air thick with the promise of a downpour. The oppressive humidity clung to everything, making the world feel as though it was holding its breath, waiting for the skies to break open. Sheriff John Landry could feel the heaviness in the air as he drove his squad car down the narrow, winding roads that cut through the heart of the bayou. The windows were down, but the air offered no relief, just the smell of wet earth and the distant tang of ozone from the lightning that flashed intermittently on the horizon.

John had one final stop to make before he could head back to the station and batten down the hatches for the storm. He was off to see Daryl Jacobs, a man who had more reason than most to wish for vengeance. Daryl's brother, John Boy, had been murdered—a brutal, killing that had shaken the small community to its core. The sheriff knew the rumours were flying fast and furious, whispers in the dark that one of the victims' families had taken justice into their own hands. But John had spoken to each of them, looked into their eyes, and he was here now to reassure Daryl that none of those families had anything to do with his brother's death.

As John pulled up at Daryl's Swamp Tours, the first fat drops of rain began to fall, splattering against the windshield with a sound like pebbles hitting the glass. He could see Daryl sitting on the porch, a cigarette hanging loosely from his lips, his eyes fixed on in the distance as if he could see something beyond the gathering storm.

Landry stepped out of the car and adjusted his hat against the rain that was quickly intensifying. The rumble of thunder rolled in from the distance, a low, ominous growl that promised a long day ahead. He walked up the steps of the porch, his boots echoing dully against the wood, and tipped his hat to the young woman sitting beside Daryl, wearing a pair of skimpy shorts and a figure-hugging t-shirt that did little to hide the curves beneath. Her eyes met John's with a mixture of curiosity and defiance, but she said nothing, just continued to tap her nails against the arm of her chair.

"Morning, Daryl," he greeted, his voice steady, though the storm was threatening to drown it out. "Mind if I have a word?"

Daryl took a long drag on his cigarette, the tip glowing brightly in the gathering darkness, then nodded toward the empty chair across from him. "Ain't got much else to do, Sheriff. No swamp tours today, with this weather coming in."

Landry nodded and took the seat, the old wood creaking under his weight. The rain was falling in earnest now, drumming against the roof of the porch, creating a wall of sound that isolated them from the rest of the world.

"I came by to talk about John Boy," Landry began, his voice low but firm. "I know you said about how maybe one of the victims' families had something to do with what happened to him. I wanted to let you know I've spoken to them all, and I'm certain none of them took retribution."

Daryl's gaze flicked over to Landry, his expression unreadable. "You sure about that, Sheriff?"

"I'm sure," Landry replied. He leaned forward, elbows resting on his knees as he met Daryl's gaze head-on. "Olivia Sims only has her mother, and that woman works all hours just to keep a roof over their heads. She doesn't have the time or the means to do what was done to your brother."

"And Charlotte Franklin?" Daryl asked, his voice carrying a note of challenge. "She's got those grandparents of hers, and from what I hear, they're tough old birds."

"They're tough, but they're old and frail," Landry countered gently. "They're more concerned with making sure Charlotte's future is secure. I don't think they've got it in them to seek out revenge, not like that."

"And what about the Knights? They've got money, and connections could've hired someone to do it."

Sheriff Landry shook his head. "I had a good chat with Emma Knight's parents. They're devastated, but they're not the kind of people who would take the law into their own hands. They just don't have it in them to do what happened to your brother."

Daryl was silent for a long moment, his eyes searching Landry's face for something, anything that might hint at a lie. But all he found was the sheriff's steady, unyielding gaze.

"So what are you saying, Sheriff?" Daryl finally asked, his voice rough around the edges. "That whoever killed John Boy is still out there? That you don't have any leads?"

Landry's jaw tightened. This was the hardest part, the part where he had to admit that justice hadn't yet been served. "I'm saying that I'm doing everything I can to find out who did this, Daryl. And when I do, they'll face the full weight of the law."

Daryl crushed his cigarette under his boot and stood, his eyes flashing with something dark, something dangerous. "You better, Sheriff. Because if you don't find him soon, I will."

The rain fell harder, the thunder rolling in overhead, a reminder that the storm was far from over. Sheriff Landry rose from his chair, nodding once to Daryl before tipping his hat to the young woman. "Good evening, ma'am."

She smiled and watched him with those blue eyes as he made his way back to his car, the rain drenching him in seconds. He climbed in, started the engine, and drove away, the headlights cutting through the thickening gloom.

As he headed back toward town, the storm finally broke, the sky opening in a deluge that turned the world into a blur of water and lightning. Sheriff John Landry knew the storm wouldn't be the only thing raging in his small town tonight. The real tempest was brewing in the hearts of men like Daryl Jacobs, and it was only a matter of time before it unleashed its fury.

But for now, all he could do was drive through the rain, the weight of unsolved murders pressing down on him as heavily as the storm clouds above.

CHAPTER SEVEN

Sheriff John Landry gripped the steering wheel tightly, his knuckles white against the dark leather. The storm was relentless, with rain hammering against the windshield, the sound almost deafening. The wipers flailed back and forth at their highest setting, but the wall of water coming down from the heavens made it nearly impossible to see more than a few feet ahead. Every flash of lightning illuminated the road in stark, blinding white, only to be swallowed again by the darkness. The wind howled, pushing against the vehicle, making it sway ever so slightly as Landry drove through the rural backroads.

Each mile back to Houma felt like a small victory, the comforting knowledge of the station's warm, dry interior keeping him going. His eyes darted from the road to the rearview mirror, half-expecting the shadows outside to come to life in the storm. The nervous energy from the recent crime scene still buzzed through his veins. He had seen a lot in his years as sheriff, but this case—it gnawed at him in a way few others had.

Finally, the familiar shape of the Houma Police Station loomed ahead, a small fortress of brick and mortar against the fury of the elements. Landry pulled into the parking lot and switched off the engine. For a moment, he sat in the car, listening to the rain battering the roof, gathering his thoughts. He knew what awaited inside—more questions than answers, more mysteries than solutions.

Bracing himself, he opened the car door. The rain assaulted him immediately, drenching his clothes in the mere seconds it took to slam the door shut and dash the ten yards to the station entrance. By the time he reached the sanctuary of the foyer, he was soaked to the skin, water dripping from his hat and running down his face in cold rivulets.

"Goddamn storm," he muttered to himself, shaking off as much water as he could before stepping into the warmth of the station.

Inside, the lights were dim, the usual early morning quiet only interrupted by the hum of the air conditioning and the distant clatter of typewriters from the records room. Landry wiped his brow and strode toward his office, peeling off his soaked jacket and tossing it over a chair. Before getting changed, he had one task on his mind.

"Mike!" he called out, his voice carrying through the station.

Deputy Mike Harris, the youngest of his team, appeared in the hallway a moment later, looking up from a stack of paperwork. "Sheriff?"

"Get over here," Landry said, pulling a dry shirt from the locker in his office. "I need you to do something for me."

As Harris approached, Landry unbuttoned his soggy shirt and continued, "I want you to look into something. See if there have been any other decapitated murders in Louisiana over the last few years."

Harris raised an eyebrow, surprised by the unusual request, but nodded without hesitation. "You think there's a pattern, Sheriff?"

"Just a hunch," Landry said, pulling on the fresh shirt. "This one feels different. Check it out."

Harris hurried off to the records room, and Landry settled into his chair, the familiar creak of the old leather a small comfort. The storm outside showed no signs of letting up, the rain continuing to pelt the windows with relentless fury. He leaned back, running a hand through his damp hair, and closed his eyes for a moment, trying to push away the image of the crime scene that had been seared into his memory.

A few minutes later, Harris returned, a thin file in hand. "Sheriff, you were right. There've been four other cases in the last seven years. All unsolved. All decapitations."

Landry sat up, suddenly alert. "Where?"

Harris spread the file on the desk, revealing a map of Louisiana with four red dots marking the locations. "First The first one was in Baton Rouge, seven years ago. Male, thirty-five years old. Next, Lafayette, five years ago, a sixty-two-year-old male. Then Monroe, two years ago, a young man, just twenty-two. And the last one was in Jackson, last year. Black male, fifty-three years old."

Landry frowned, tracing the dots with his finger. "Any connection between the victims?"

"None that stands out," Harris admitted. "Different backgrounds, different professions. They were all found in public places, but there's no clear link between them."

Landry stared at the map, his mind racing. Four unsolved murders, all with the same brutal method of killing, scattered across the state. The dates didn't suggest a clear pattern, but the locations—they formed a rough circle, with Houma right in the middle.

"Looks like we got ourselves a serial killer," Landry said, more to himself than to Harris. The thought sent a chill down his spine, despite the warmth of the station. "And he's been at it for years."

Harris looked at him, eyes wide with a mix of fear and determination. "What do we do, Sheriff?"

Landry leaned back, his gaze never leaving the map. "We start digging. I want to know everything about these cases. Who the victims were, what they were doing, who they knew."

Harris nodded, already mentally cataloguing the tasks ahead. "Yes, sir."

As the young deputy left to begin his research, Landry sat in the quiet of his office, the storm outside a distant roar now. The case had just taken a dark turn, and he knew this was only the beginning. The killer was out there, somewhere, and Landry was determined to find him before another life was taken.

The storm would pass, but the darkness this case brought with it—it would linger, hovering over Houma like a shadow.

CHAPTER EIGHT

Deputy Mike Harris sat at his desk in the Houma Police Station, the glow of his computer screen illuminating the dark corners of the room. The storm outside had subsided, leaving behind a thick blanket of humidity that clung to everything. But Mike barely noticed; he was too engrossed in the files spread out before him. These were no ordinary cases—they were a chilling series of unsolved murders, each with a brutal commonality that sent a shiver down his spine.

He took a deep breath and opened the first file.

Case 1: David Jones - Baton Rouge

David Jones, age thirty-five, had once been a respected businessman in Baton Rouge. But that all changed when he was charged with sexual assault, accused of raping a woman he had met through a mutual friend. The case went to trial, but Jones was acquitted, and the charges were dropped due to insufficient evidence and a strong defence that discredited the victim's testimony. Despite the court's ruling, the public's opinion was harsh; whispers of guilt followed him everywhere.

Jones tried to move on, but the stain on his reputation lingered. Then, just a few months after his acquittal,

Jones was found dead in his own home. The details were grisly—his body lay on the living room floor, and his head was missing. The police report noted that there were no signs of forced entry, no signs of struggle. The scene was eerily clean, as if the killer had been in no rush, and had taken their time. The case shocked the community, but despite an intense investigation, no leads ever materialised. The case grew cold, and Baton Rouge tried to forget.

Mike felt a knot tighten in his stomach as he closed the file. The brutality of Jones' murder contrasted sharply with the clean image of a man acquitted by the law but not by society.

Case 2: Jack Johnson - Lafayette

The second file belonged to Jack Johnson, a sixty-two-year-old man from Lafayette. Johnson had been a retired schoolteacher, known for his stern demeanour and rigid discipline. But his world unravelled when he was accused of molesting a student—a teenage boy who had attended his maths class. The trial had been long and painful, with the boy's testimony wavering under cross-examination. In the end, Johnson was found not guilty, his defence painting the accuser as a troubled youth seeking revenge.

Though he had been exonerated in court, Johnson's reputation never recovered. He lived the remainder of his days in isolation, until one day, he simply disappeared. Days later, a hiker found his body in a dense patch of undergrowth outside Lafayette. Like Jones, Johnson's head was missing, the cut clean and precise. There were no other wounds, no signs of a struggle. The case was eerily like Jones', and yet, investigators failed to connect the dots. The file was thin—few leads, fewer answers.

Mike frowned as he studied the scant evidence. It was as though the killer had taken pleasure in not just the act itself, but in the complete elusiveness afterward.

Case 3: Mike Williams - Monroe

The third file detailed the murder of Mike Williams, a twenty-two-year-old from Monroe. Williams had a chequered past, including several run-ins with the law for minor offences—vandalism, and public intoxication. But it was an accusation of attempted rape that nearly destroyed him. Williams had been charged with attacking a local woman outside a bar, but after a messy trial, he was acquitted. The case hinged on shaky witness testimonies, and in the end, Williams walked free.

The freedom was short-lived. Less than a month after his acquittal, Williams' body was discovered in the parking lot of a notorious biker bar on the outskirts of Monroe. His head, like the others, was gone. The investigation went nowhere—witnesses were uncooperative, and the rough crowd that frequented the bar had no love for the police. The case was shelved, another unsolved mystery in a town full of them.

Mike couldn't shake the feeling that these were no random killings. There was something methodical, almost surgical, about the way the murders had been carried out. And yet, the connection between the victims wasn't clear—until he reached the last file.

Case 4: Robert Brown - Jackson

The final file was the most recent. Robert Brown, a fifty-three-year-old black man from Jackson, Mississippi. Brown had lived a hard life, scraping by with odd jobs and manual labour. He was charged with aggravated assault, accused of severely beating a young white boy during a confrontation in his neighbourhood. The case became highly charged, tensions flaring in the community. But in court, Brown was acquitted—the jury finding found that the boy had provoked the attack, and Brown had acted in self-defence.

Despite the acquittal, Brown was shunned, and seen as a dangerous man who had escaped justice. Months later, his body was found in his garage, his head missing just like the others. The crime scene was once again disturbingly clean, devoid of evidence or clues. Local police had little to go on, and as time passed, the case faded into the background.

Mike stared at the four files spread out before him. The pattern was undeniable: all men, all acquitted of serious crimes, and all brutally murdered afterward. Their heads were taken; their lives ended in a way that suggested someone was out there delivering their own twisted form of justice.

But who was it? And why? These were the questions that now haunted Mike Harris. He knew he had to dig deeper, to find the connections that others had missed. As he gathered the files, preparing to brief Sheriff Landry, a sense of unease settled over him. Whoever was behind these killings was not only careful but also deeply motivated by something darker than simple revenge.

CHAPTER NINE

Deputy Mike Harris stood outside Sheriff Landry's office, the weight of the files in his hands almost too much to bear. The thick folders contained his findings — painstakingly gathered evidence and connections that pointed to a grim and unsettling truth. The air felt heavy with tension, each breath dragging in a sense of dread. He knew what he had uncovered, and he knew how Sheriff Landry would react.

With a deep breath, Mike knocked on the door and entered. The office was dimly lit, the afternoon sun casting long shadows across the room. Sheriff Landry sat behind his cluttered desk, the lines on his weathered face deepened by the stress of the last few months. The sheriff looked up as Mike stepped in, his eyes sharp, reflecting a mix of curiosity and concern.

"Mike," Landry said, gesturing to the chair in front of him. "What've you got for me?"

Mike hesitated for a moment, then stepped forward and placed the thick files on the desk. "Sheriff, I've been looking into any decapitation cases. You asked me to look into it."

Landry leaned back in his chair, folding his arms. "Yeah, what did you find out?"

Mike opened the files and spread out several photographs and documents. "I've found something… something big. Each of those victims was acquitted of their crime, and they were all men who got off on technicalities or had insufficient evidence to convict. But, Sheriff, each one of them was guilty as sin, I'm sure of it."

Landry's eyes narrowed as he leaned forward, studying the evidence laid out before him. "And you're telling me these four men, all acquitted criminals, were targeted by the same person?"

"Maybe," Mike said, his voice firm. "I've found patterns in the killings. The decapitations weren't just random; they were methodical, almost ritualistic. Whoever is doing this is very precise, leaving no traceable evidence. This person is executing them—literally—in a way that suggests they're delivering their own twisted form of justice."

Landry picked up one of the photos, the image of a headless body still gruesome despite the number of times he'd seen it. He set it back down, exhaling slowly. "Damn it, Mike. This is bigger than anything we've dealt with before."

Mike nodded, his face grave. "That's what I'm afraid of. This isn't just some psycho with a knife, Sheriff. This is a serial killer, and he's following a code. He's picking off people who escaped justice, and he's doing it with surgical precision. We're way out of our depth here."

Landry was silent for a moment, the weight of the situation sinking in. He rubbed a hand over his face, the weariness of years in law enforcement showing. Finally, he looked up at Mike, his voice low and serious.

"We can't handle this alone, Mike. This is too big for us, too well-planned. Whoever this is, they've covered their tracks so well we didn't even see it until now. We've got a serial killer on our hands, one who thinks he's some sort of vigilante. We need to call in reinforcements—this is a job for the FBI."

Mike felt a strange mix of relief and apprehension. Relief that Landry recognized the severity of the situation, but apprehension because bringing in the FBI meant this was real, that it was no longer just his hunch or investigation. It was a full-blown serial killer case.

"I'll make the call," Landry continued, already reaching for the phone. "But, Mike, until they get here, we keep this under wraps. No one outside this room knows what we've found. The last thing we need is a panic on our hands."

"Understood, Sheriff," Mike replied, though his mind was already racing ahead, thinking about the next steps, the possible dangers, and the fact that a killer was out there, watching, waiting for his next target.

As Landry began speaking into the phone, relaying the situation to someone on the other end, Mike's eyes drifted back to the file on the desk. Each victim, their stories unfinished, their deaths unresolved.

The sheriff was right—this was too big for them. But even as the FBI prepared to descend on their small town, Mike couldn't shake the feeling that they were already too late. The killer was out there, and he wasn't finished yet.

As he left the office, the door closing softly behind him, Mike felt the weight of the case settle on his shoulders once more. Reinforcements were coming, but the clock was ticking, and in the shadows of the town, justice—twisted, dark, and merciless—was waiting to strike again.

CHAPTER TEN

Agent Enzo Romano stood at the grill, the smoky aroma of sizzling steaks and sausages filling the air around him. His dark, curly hair was slightly tousled from the river breeze, and his olive-toned skin glistened in the late afternoon sun. Enzo was a striking figure—tall, broad-shouldered, with a presence that commanded respect but exuded warmth. His Italian heritage was evident in his chiselled features, deep brown eyes that could flash with intensity or soften with affection, and an easy smile that had charmed many over the years.

Behind him, the Romano household was alive with the sounds of laughter and conversation. The sprawling house on the riverbank was a testament to Enzo's years of hard work and dedication. The large, white-painted colonial-style home was surrounded by lush greenery, its broad porch offering a perfect view of the river. A wooden jetty extended out into the water, where a couple of jet skis bobbed gently. This place was his sanctuary, a refuge from the darkness he often encountered in his line of work.

As Enzo turned the steaks, flipping them with practised ease, his wife, Maria, approached, carrying a tray of freshly prepared salad. Maria was as much the heart of this home as Enzo was. Petite but strong, with warm brown eyes and a nurturing demeanour, she managed their household with the same precision and care that Enzo applied to his investigations. They had met in college, and since then, their lives had become deeply intertwined. Together, they had built a life full of love, laughter, and two beautiful children.

"How's it going, Chef?" Maria teased, placing the salad on the nearby table.

Enzo grinned, his eyes twinkling. "Just about perfect, amore. These steaks are going to be the talk of the neighbourhood."

Nearby, their two kids—Alessia, aged ten, and Luca, aged eight—were playing with a group of friends, their laughter carrying across the yard. Enzo watched them for a moment, a sense of pride and contentment washing over him. This was what he lived for—his family, and their happiness.

"Don't get too comfortable, Romeo," a voice called out from behind him. Enzo turned to see his FBI partner, Lisa Rodriguez, walking toward him, a teasing smile on her face.

Lisa was a sharp, no-nonsense agent who had risen through the ranks alongside Enzo. Born and raised in New York, Lisa had a fiery personality to match her raven-black hair, which she always wore pulled back in a tight ponytail. Her quick wit and unrelenting determination had earned her a reputation as one of the best in the Bureau. She had a knack for getting to the truth, no matter how deep it was buried. Today, though, she was off duty, dressed casually in jeans and a fitted blouse, her guard down for the first time in weeks.

"Lisa, I thought I was the one supposed to give you a hard time," Enzo shot back, laughing. "How's your new boyfriend holding up?"

Lisa rolled her eyes but couldn't hide the slight blush that crept up her cheeks. She gestured over her shoulder to a tall, athletic-looking man standing by the porch. "That's Derek. We've been dating for three weeks, and I think I might've scared him off with all the 'war stories' from work. But he's hanging in there."

Enzo chuckled. "Poor guy doesn't know what he's gotten himself into, does he?"

"Not a clue," Lisa replied, but there was a softness in her tone that hinted at something deeper. For all her toughness, Lisa was still figuring out how to balance her fierce independence with the desire for companionship. Enzo had seen her go through a few relationships, but there was something different about how she talked about Derek. He wondered if maybe, just maybe, this one would stick.

The sound of Enzo's phone buzzing on the table interrupted their banter. He frowned, wiping his hands on a towel before picking it up. Lisa's phone buzzed a moment later, and the look they exchanged was one of mutual understanding. Calls from headquarters during a family barbecue were never good news.

Enzo answered, and the voice on the other end was brisk, all business. "Romano, we need you and Rodriguez on a plane immediately. We've got a situation in Houma, Louisiana. Multiple murders—decapitations. Looks like the work of a serial killer. Pack your bags. You're off to Houma."

Enzo's expression hardened as he listened to the details, his mind already shifting gears from family man to FBI agent. "Understood," he said curtly before ending the call.

Lisa was already on the phone with her own contact, her demeanour mirroring Enzo's as she got the same briefing. When she hung up, she turned to him, her face set in grim determination. "Looks like the fun's over."

Enzo nodded, his jaw tight. "Yeah. We've got a serial killer on the loose. Time to get to work."

Maria, who had been watching from a distance, approached, concern etched on her face. "Enzo?"

He turned to her, his eyes softening. "I'm sorry, Maria. I have to go. It's serious."

She nodded, her hand reaching up to cup his cheek. "I know. Just… be careful, okay?"

He leaned down, pressing a kiss to her forehead. "Always."

As he quickly packed a bag, Enzo couldn't help but glance out at the river, the peaceful scene a stark contrast to the chaos he was about to face. The jetty, the house, the life he had built here—it all felt so far away now. But this was his job, his duty. He had to protect families like his own from the darkness that lurked in the world.

Lisa and Derek were saying their goodbyes as well, and Enzo noted the brief hug they shared before Lisa turned back to him, all business once more. "You ready?" she asked, her voice steady.

"Let's do this," Enzo replied, slinging his bag over his shoulder.

As they walked toward the driveway, Maria and Derek watching them go, Enzo felt a familiar surge of adrenaline. The peaceful afternoon had given way to the cold reality of their work, but he knew they were ready. This was what they did—hunt down monsters and bring them to justice.

But as they headed toward the airport, Enzo couldn't shake the feeling that this case was different. Darker. More personal. And as the plane took off into the night, he glanced over at Lisa, who seemed lost in her thoughts. They both knew this case would test them in ways they hadn't been tested before. The tranquil riverside was far behind them now, and ahead lay Houma—a place where death had taken on a new, twisted form.

CHAPTER ELEVEN

The plane touched down at Louis Armstrong New Orleans International Airport just past midnight. Agents Enzo Romano and Lisa Rodriguez stepped off the plane into the thick, humid air, the remnants of a recent storm still lingering in the atmosphere. The drive from the airport to Houma took a little over an hour, with Enzo at the wheel. The highway was mostly empty at this late hour, illuminated only by the occasional streetlamp and the headlights of their rented SUV. The storm had passed, but the roads were still slick, and the trees on either side of the road dripped with rainwater.

As they approached Houma, the air grew heavier with the scent of wet earth and the lingering musk of the bayou. The town was quiet, save for the faint sounds of water trickling through the nearby swamps and the distant croak of frogs. The storm had left its mark—fallen branches littered the streets, and puddles of rainwater reflected the pale light of the moon.

They finally reached their destination: a small, nondescript motel on the outskirts of town. The neon sign flickered intermittently, casting an eerie glow over the parking lot. The motel was a simple, two-storey building with peeling paint and a few dimly lit windows. It wasn't much, but it was functional—a place to rest and regroup before the gruelling work ahead.

Enzo parked the SUV in front of the motel office, the tyres crunching over the gravel. He and Lisa stepped out, the night air pressing down on them like a damp blanket. The sound of cicadas buzzed in the background, blending with the faint rustle of leaves.

"Looks like we're the only ones here," Lisa remarked, glancing around the deserted lot.

"Not surprising," Enzo replied, his voice low. "Houma isn't exactly a tourist hotspot, especially after a storm like that."

They entered the motel office, where a bored-looking clerk with a thinning comb-over and a name tag that read "Pete" barely looked up from his television. Enzo handled the check-in, and within minutes, Pete handed them two keys, each attached to a worn plastic fob.

"Rooms 12 and 13," Pete said, his voice a dull monotone. "End of the boardwalk. If you need anything, just pick up the phone. I'll be here all night."

"Thanks," Enzo muttered, taking the keys. He passed one to Lisa, who gave a nod of acknowledgment.

They made their way back outside, down the narrow boardwalk, their footsteps echoing on the wooden planks. The motel smelled faintly of mildew and cleaning supplies, the kind of place where time seemed to stand still. They reached their rooms—two adjacent rooms at the far end of the motel, the numbers barely visible on the scratched brass plates.

Enzo unlocked his door and pushed it open, the hinges creaking in protest. The room was as basic as they came—two twin beds with faded floral bedspreads, a small wooden dresser, and a television that looked like it hadn't been used in years. The wallpaper was peeling in the corners, and the carpet was worn and stained. But the beds were made, and the air conditioning hummed quietly, offering some relief from the sticky night air.

"Not exactly five-star," Lisa quipped, standing in her doorway.

"No, but it'll do," Enzo replied, managing a small smile. "We'll be up early anyway."

Lisa nodded; her usual sharpness softened by exhaustion. "Yeah. We've got a long day ahead."

"Get some rest," Enzo said. "We'll regroup in the morning. Goodnight, Lisa."

"Goodnight, Enzo."

They each entered their rooms, the doors clicking shut behind them. Enzo tossed his bag onto the chair by the window and sat down on the edge of the bed. He ran a hand through his hair, the day's events catching up with him all at once. The urgency of the case, the quick departure from home, and now the strange, unsettling quiet of this small Louisiana town—it all weighed heavily on him.

He pulled out his phone and dialled Maria's number. She answered after a few rings, her voice warm and reassuring despite the late hour.

"Enzo, you made it," she said, relief evident in her tone.

"Yeah, we're here," he replied, his voice softening. "It's… well, it's Houma. Small, quiet, humid as hell."

Maria chuckled softly. "Sounds about right. How's Lisa?"

"She's good. Tired, like me. We've got a long day tomorrow, so I just wanted to call and say goodnight."

"Thank you," Maria said, her voice tender. "I miss you already."

"I miss you too. Give the kids a kiss for me in the morning, okay?"

"I will. Be safe, Enzo."

"I will. I love you."

"Love you too."

Enzo ended the call and sat for a moment, staring at the dark screen. Then he stood, kicked off his shoes, and lay down on the bed, letting the cool air from the AC wash over him. But sleep didn't come easily. His mind was already turning over the case, the details he knew so far, and the many more that would come in the days ahead.

Next door, Lisa was having a similar struggle. She sat cross-legged on her bed, her phone in her lap, staring at Derek's number. After a moment, she took a deep breath and dialled.

"Lisa," Derek answered, his voice groggy with sleep. "Is everything okay?"

"Yeah," she said, her voice quieter than usual. "I'm sorry to wake you. I just… I wanted to hear your voice."

"I'm glad you called," he said, sounding more awake now. "How's Houma?"

"Dark, humid, and quiet," she replied, forcing a small laugh. "We just got here, checked into some crappy motel. I'll be working all day tomorrow, so I just wanted to call and say goodnight."

"I'm glad you did," Derek said, his voice soft and reassuring. "Take care of yourself, okay?"

"Always," she replied. "Goodnight, Derek."

"Goodnight, Lisa."

She hung up and lay back on the bed, staring up at the ceiling. The room was silent, save for the hum of the air conditioner. She closed her eyes, trying to push thoughts of the case out of her mind, but it was no use. The weight of the task ahead pressed down on her, and she knew sleep would be a long time coming.

In the quiet of the night, both agents lay awake, their thoughts drifting between the loved ones they had left behind and the dark work that awaited them in Houma.

CHAPTER TWELVE

At precisely 7:00 AM, Agents Enzo Romano and Lisa Rodriguez emerged from the small, weathered motel into the humid Louisiana morning. The air was thick and warm, still heavy from the storm that had passed through the night before. The sky was a pale grey, promising more heat as the day wore on.

They drove in silence, the SUV's tires humming along the damp road as they made their way into town. Houma was slowly waking up, the streets starting to come alive with the day's early risers. The two agents were alert but tired, their minds still lingering on the restless sleep they'd had the night before.

As they approached the centre of town, Enzo spotted a food wagon parked on the corner of a busy intersection. The sign above the window read "Miss Ida's Cajun Delights," and a small crowd of locals was already lined up for breakfast. Enzo slowed the car and glanced over at Lisa.

"Coffee and something to eat?" he suggested.

Lisa nodded, grateful for the suggestion. "Absolutely. I could use a caffeine boost."

Enzo pulled over, and they both got out, joining the queue. The smell of sizzling bacon and freshly brewed coffee filled the air, making their stomachs rumble. When they reached the window, Miss Ida herself greeted them with a warm smile. She was an older woman with a round face and kind eyes, her greying hair tucked under a bright red bandana.

"Morning, y'all," she said cheerfully. "What can I get for you?"

"Two coffees, black, and a couple of breakfast sandwiches," Enzo replied, returning her smile.

"Comin' right up, sugar," Miss Ida said as she turned to prepare their order.

As they waited, Enzo and Lisa leaned against the side of the truck, watching the town come to life. It was a small place, with a close-knit feel—everyone seemed to know each other, exchanging greetings as they passed. It was hard to imagine that such a peaceful town could be the scene of something so dark.

Miss Ida handed them their coffees and sandwiches in brown paper bags. "Y'all enjoy now," she said with a wink.

"Thanks, ma'am," Lisa said, flashing a quick smile as they headed back to the SUV.

They ate their breakfast on the drive to the Houma Police Station, the warm food and strong coffee working their way through the last remnants of sleepiness. The town's small police station was a modest brick building with a few patrol cars parked outside. It was a far cry from the large, bustling headquarters they were used to in the city, but it had a certain charm—no-nonsense, straightforward, like the people who worked there.

Enzo parked the SUV and they walked inside, the cool air-conditioning a welcome relief from the oppressive humidity outside. The station was quiet, with a few officers at their desks, busy with the morning's paperwork. Enzo approached the front desk, where a young officer with a buzz cut and a crisp uniform looked up at them.

"Morning," Enzo said, flashing his badge. "Agents Romano and Rodriguez. We're here to see Sheriff Landry."

The officer nodded. "Sheriff's not in yet, but he's on his way. You can wait in the conference room. I'll let him know you're here."

"Thanks," Lisa said as they followed the officer down the hall.

They were shown to a small conference room with a large table in the centre and a whiteboard on one wall. The room was plain but functional, with a few chairs around the table and a couple of windows looking out onto the parking lot. Enzo and Lisa sat down, their expressions focused and serious.

Meanwhile, across town, Sheriff Landry was rudely awakened by the shrill ring of his phone. He groaned, rolling over to squint at the clock on his nightstand. 7:55 AM. Too early for any sane person to be up, he thought, as he fumbled for the phone.

"This better be important," he grumbled into the receiver.

"It's Mike down at the station, Sheriff," came the reply. "Those FBI agents are here. They're waiting for you."

Landry sighed, the weight of the day settling on him. "Alright, Mike. Tell them I'll be there in twenty minutes."

He hung up and dragged himself out of bed, muttering to himself as he made his way to the bathroom. Landry was a big man, with a broad frame that had gone a bit soft over the years, and a face that was often set in a permanent scowl. His hair was thinning and greying at the temples, and his deep-set eyes were a little bloodshot from the restless night he'd had.

He showered quickly, the cold water shocking him fully awake. Once dressed in his uniform, he grabbed a glass of orange juice from the fridge, gulping it down in a few quick swallows. He was out the door and in his cruiser within minutes, heading toward the station.

Landry pulled into the station parking lot, his mood still sour from the early wake-up call. He was not a morning person, and he liked his routine—slow mornings with a pot of coffee and the newspaper. But there was no time for that today. The FBI was here.

He walked into the station and headed straight for the conference room. As he opened the door, he saw the two agents sitting at the table, their expressions alert and professional.

"Morning, Sheriff," Enzo said, rising to shake his hand.

"Morning," Landry grunted, accepting the handshake with a firm grip. He turned to Lisa and shook her hand as well. "Agent Rodriguez."

"Thanks for meeting us so early," Lisa said, noting the sheriff's less-than-enthusiastic demeanour.

Landry waved it off, gesturing for them to sit. "No problem. Just not used to getting up this early unless it's hunting season."

He took a seat at the head of the table, folding his large hands in front of him. "So, you're here about these murders. I'm sure you've already been briefed on the basics, but let me fill you in on the latest. We had another one two nights ago. John Boy Adams—local tour guide. We found him floating in the swamp, decapitated like the others."

Landry's voice was gruff, but there was a tinge of weariness in it, the kind that comes from seeing too much death up close. "Whoever's doing this, they're smart. No evidence, no witnesses, just clean kills. It's like they know exactly what they're doing."

He reached into a drawer and pulled out the files, sliding them across the table to the agents. "These are all the case files on the unsolved murders. Startin' with the first one seven years ago. Same MO, same damn mystery."

Enzo and Lisa exchanged a glance before opening the files. The room fell silent as they began to sift through the documents, their eyes scanning over the gruesome details of each case. Photos of crime scenes, autopsy reports, witness statements—every piece of the puzzle laid out in front of them.

Landry leaned back in his chair, watching them work. "This isn't your usual serial killer," he said quietly. "This one… this one's different. You'll see it in the files. They've been targeting' people who… who've been acquitted in court on, let's say unsavoury charges. But that doesn't mean they deserved this."

Enzo looked up from the file he was reading. "We've been briefed on the possibility that this is some kind of vigilante. Someone who's taking justice into their own hands."

"Yeah, that's the theory," Landry said, rubbing his temples. "But it's more than just theory now. We need to stop this before it happens again."

Lisa closed the file she was holding and looked at Landry. "We're here to help, Sheriff. We'll do whatever it takes to bring this person to justice."

Landry nodded; , his face grim. "I sure hope so, Agent. Because if you don't, I'm not sure anyone else will."

CHAPTER THIRTEEN

The engine of Daryl Jacobs' old pickup rumbled as it rolled over the gravel road that led to the local store. The sun hung low in the sky, casting long shadows across the quiet neighbourhood. The town was small, the kind where everyone knew each other's business, and where secrets were buried deep but never forgotten. Daryl had been on edge ever since his brother's death—a senseless, brutal murder that had left the entire community shaken.

As he drove, Daryl's mind raced, replaying the events of the past few weeks. His brother, John Boy, had been found dead in the swamp, head missing. The police had no leads, or at least that's what they claimed. But Daryl wasn't convinced. He knew John Boy had a habit of getting into trouble, always looking at the young girls. But he was also fiercely loyal and had a heart bigger than anyone Daryl knew. Whoever did this to him had to pay.

He was pulled from his thoughts as he passed Olivia Simms' house, the creaking old structure sitting at the edge of town. Olivia's mother, Mrs. Simms, stood out front, her weathered face etched with lines that told stories of hardship and resilience. But it wasn't her that caught Daryl's attention—it was the two men standing with her. They were big, muscular, and unfamiliar, their dark skin glistening in the late afternoon sun. Daryl's grip on the steering wheel tightened.

As he slowed the truck down to a crawl, his heart began to pound in his chest. He had heard whispers about strangers in town, about men who didn't belong and who brought trouble with them. These two fit the description. Their clothes were neat, but there was something dangerous about them, something in the way they carried themselves. One of them had a scar running down his left cheek, the other a tattoo that snaked up his neck and disappeared into his shirt collar. They looked like men who had seen violence—who were capable of it.

Mrs. Simms seemed to be talking animatedly, her hands gesturing wildly. The men listened, but their eyes were cold, emotionless. When Daryl's truck approached, the men turned their heads in unison, locking eyes with him. A chill ran down his spine. For a moment, the world seemed to stop as they stared at each other. Daryl felt like a deer caught in the headlights, exposed and vulnerable.

The man with the scar narrowed his eyes, his gaze piercing. Daryl couldn't shake the feeling that these were the men he had been looking for, the ones who might have taken his brother's life. He felt a surge of anger, hot and fierce, but it was tempered by a sliver of fear. They looked like they could tear him apart without breaking a sweat. But then, he was his brother's keeper, and he wasn't about to back down.

Daryl's foot hovered over the gas pedal, his instincts screaming at him to drive away, to put distance between himself and the menacing figures. But another part of him, the part that demanded justice for John Boy, urged him to stop, to confront them right there. Before he could decide, the man with the tattoo smirked, a cold, knowing smile that made Daryl's blood run cold.

It was as if they knew what he was thinking, as if they were daring him to do something about it. Daryl's breath hitched, his pulse quickening. He couldn't face them alone—not yet. There was a time for reckoning, but it wasn't now. He wasn't prepared. He needed to gather his wits, and more importantly, he needed backup.

He pressed down on the gas, and the truck surged forward, the tires spitting gravel as he sped away. In the rearview mirror, he saw the men watching him, their figures growing smaller in the distance, but their presence still looming large in his mind. Mrs. Simms seemed to continue her conversation as if nothing had happened, but Daryl couldn't shake the feeling that something sinister was brewing.

As he drove towards town, Daryl's thoughts raced. He needed to round up his mates—guys who had known his John Boy, who had loved him like a brother, and who would be willing to stand with him against whatever threat these strangers posed. He wasn't sure what he was getting himself into, but he knew one thing for certain: he wasn't going to let his brother's murder go unanswered.

He pulled out his phone and began to dial, his fingers trembling with adrenaline. There was a storm coming, and Daryl was ready to face it head-on, no matter what it took.

CHAPTER FOURTEEN

Agents Enzo Romano and Lisa Rodriguez walked out of the sheriff's office, the oppressive Louisiana heat hitting them like a wall. The sun was high, and the air was thick with the sticky, suffocating humidity that Lisa despised. It clung to her like a second skin, making her shirt stick to her back as they made their way to the SUV. Sheriff Landry had been cooperative, handing over the five case files, but Lisa couldn't shake the feeling that he was relieved to pass the burden on to someone else.

"Remind me why we're here in the middle of July again?" Lisa muttered as she slid into the passenger seat, fanning herself with a file.

"Because we drew the short straw," Enzo replied with a smirk, starting the engine. The air conditioning roared to life, providing a brief but much-needed blast of cool air.

Lisa rolled her eyes, leaning her head back against the headrest. "Next time, we're sticking to cases in places with actual seasons. This heat is unbearable."

Enzo chuckled as he navigated the narrow, winding roads that led away from the sheriff's office. "You're the one who said you wanted more fieldwork."

"Yeah, but I was thinking more along the lines of, I don't know, Seattle or maybe even Chicago in the fall. Not the middle of nowhere in Louisiana in the dead of summer." She wiped the sweat from her brow, her frustration evident.

As they drove, the landscape outside the windows blurred into a tapestry of swampland and dense forest. The roads were lined with ancient oaks draped in Spanish moss, their gnarled branches reaching out like twisted fingers. The scene might have been beautiful under different circumstances, but all Lisa could think about was getting out of the heat.

After what felt like an eternity, Enzo spotted a small diner on the side of the road— with a faded sign that read "Maggie's Diner." The place looked like it had been plucked straight out of a 1950s postcard, complete with rustic charm curtains and a neon "Open" sign flickering in the window.

"Lunch?" Enzo suggested, nodding toward the diner.

Lisa glanced at the clock on the dashboard. It was past noon, and her stomach growled in response. "Yeah, why not. I could use a break from this heat."

They pulled into the gravel parking lot, the tires crunching underfoot as they stepped out of the car. The sun bore down on them, relentlessly, as they hurried inside. The interior of the diner was cool and dimly lit, a stark contrast to the sweltering world outside. A few locals sat at the counter, nursing cups of coffee and chatting quietly.

Enzo and Lisa slid into a booth near the back, away from prying eyes. A waitress appeared almost immediately; her pencil poised above a notepad.

"What can I get y'all?" she asked with a warm smile.

"Two iced teas, please," Enzo said. "And I'll have the club sandwich."

"I'll take the Cobb salad," Lisa added, grateful for the cool air and the prospect of a cold drink.

As they waited for their food, the conversation turned to more personal matters—something Enzo had a knack for. "So, how's Derek?" he asked casually, leaning back in the booth.

Lisa couldn't help but smile at the mention of her new boyfriend. "He's good. Things are going well. He's been really understanding about my crazy schedule. We're even talking about taking a trip together next month."

"That's great. Where to?"

"Maybe the coast. Somewhere cool and breezy," she said, emphasizing the last words with a grin.

Enzo chuckled. "Sounds like you've got it all figured out."

Lisa shrugged, but her smile widened. It felt good to talk about something normal, something that wasn't related to the gruesome case files sitting in the SUV outside.

Their food arrived, and they ate quickly, knowing they had work to do. The small talk was a welcome distraction, but the weight of their assignment hung over them like a storm cloud.

After lunch, they stepped back outside, and the heat hit them again, a relentless wave of humidity that felt even worse after the brief respite. Lisa let out a groan as they climbed back into the SUV.

"Back into the furnace," she muttered, buckling her seatbelt.

Enzo didn't say anything, but she could see the tension in his jaw as he started the car. They both knew that lunch had been a temporary escape from the grim reality of why they were here.

The drive to the motel was quiet, the earlier levity evaporating as their thoughts turned back to the reason they were in Louisiana. Five decapitated bodies, each one more disturbing than the last, and not a single solid lead to go on. The victims had no apparent connection to each other—different ages, different backgrounds, different parts of the state. Yet the brutality of the crimes suggested a pattern, someone delivering their own justice in a horrific way.

Back at the no-frills, budget Motel on the outskirts of town, the kind of place where people didn't ask questions. They parked in front of Enzo's room and grabbed the files from the back seat.

Inside, the room was small but clean, with two twin beds and a rickety table that wobbled when Enzo set down the stack of case files. Lisa kicked off her shoes and sat cross-legged on one of the beds, spreading out the files in front of her.

"Let's see what we're dealing with," Enzo said, pulling out his notebook and pen.

They worked in silence for a while, flipping through pages of autopsy reports, crime scene photos, and witness statements. The details were grisly, each file more horrifying than the last. But as Lisa pored over the documents, something began to nag at the back of her mind—a name that kept appearing, not in the victim's section, but elsewhere.

"Enzo, look at this," she said suddenly, holding up a file. "Each of these victims was prosecuted by the same district attorney. Travis Hale."

Enzo looked up from his notes, his brow furrowing. "You sure?"

Lisa nodded, her finger tracing the name on the page. "Yeah. It's here in the court records. They were all tried for various charges—nothing connected—but Hale was the DA on each case."

Enzo leaned back, considering this new information. "That's a hell of a coincidence."

"Or it's not a coincidence at all," Lisa said, her voice tinged with excitement. "This could be our first real lead."

Enzo nodded slowly, his mind already turning over the possibilities. "If Travis Hale is connected to all of this, we need to find out how. And fast."

Another storm was beginning to brew, casting long shadows across the motel room. But for the first time since they'd arrived, Lisa felt a spark of hope. The heat and the humidity might be unbearable, but they were finally getting somewhere. And they wouldn't stop until they uncovered the truth behind those five disturbing deaths.

CHAPTER FIFTEEN

The sky had darkened unnaturally fast, clouds rolling in like an ominous tide, thick and black as ink. A low rumble of thunder echoed in the distance, and the wind picked up, sending a shiver through the humid air. Enzo Romano and Lisa Rodriguez stood by the window of their motel room, watching as the storm gathered pace. Sheets of rain began to fall, tapping against the glass like impatient fingers.

"What do you think?" Enzo asked, his gaze fixed on the gathering tempest. "Should we still head to Hale's office tonight?"

Lisa shook her head, pulling her attention away from the storm outside. "No point. This weather's getting worse by the minute. We'd barely make it out of town, let alone all the way to New Orleans."

Enzo nodded in agreement, sighing as he moved away from the window. "We'll have to wait until morning. It's not worth the risk in this weather."

Lisa sat back down on the bed; the files spread out before her. She'd been going over the details they'd uncovered, trying to piece together the puzzle that was Travis Hale. "I looked him up," she said, flipping through her notes. "Travis Hale, just 38 years old. Passed with top grades at Stanford University before joining Fish and Richardson. Made partner in record time, then left to set up his own firm in Louisiana. He's been a rising star ever since. Now he's the go-to guy for prosecutions in the state, with a 90 percent conviction rate."

Enzo whistled softly, impressed despite himself. "That's one hell of a record. No wonder he's got such a reputation."

"Yeah," Lisa agreed, her brow furrowed in thought. "But it makes you wonder—why would a guy like that get tangled up in something like this? What's the connection between him and those five victims?"

Enzo rubbed his chin, deep in thought. "Good question. Maybe it's not about the victims at all. Maybe it's about something—or someone—else entirely. But we won't know until we talk to him."

Lisa's phone buzzed on the nightstand, interrupting her thoughts. She picked it up, glancing at the screen. It was a notification about the storm—flash flood warnings, severe weather alerts, the works. She grimaced, tossing the phone aside. "This storm's gonna be a real mess. Looks like we're stuck here for the night."

Enzo sighed and picked up the motel phone, dialling his office to try and schedule an appointment with Hale for the next day. After a few rings, the line connected, and he spoke briefly with his secretary, "Hey, it's Agent Romano, FBI. We would like to set up a meeting with Travis Hale tomorrow?...

"He's in court tomorrow. Final arguments in Jefferson Parish court"?

"Alright, thanks."

He hung up and turned back to Lisa. "Hale's in court tomorrow, wrapping up a case. Final arguments in Jefferson Parish."

Lisa looked up, her eyes narrowing. "Jefferson Parish? That's not too far from here."

Enzo nodded. "Yeah, I was thinking the same thing. What better way to get a read on him than to see him in action? We can head over there tomorrow, watch the proceedings, and catch him afterward."

Lisa grinned, her earlier frustration giving way to a spark of determination. "Sounds like a plan. If he's the one behind these murders—or even if he's just involved—we'll see it in the way he handles himself in court."

The rain intensified outside, hammering against the motel with a relentless fury. The wind howled, rattling the windows, and lightning lit up the sky in blinding flashes. The storm was in full swing now, a wild, uncontrollable force. But inside the motel room, the agents were focused, their minds already on the day ahead.

"Let's get some rest," Enzo said, glancing at the clock. "We've got a long day tomorrow."

Lisa nodded, but her mind was still racing, thoughts of Travis Hale swirling with the storm outside. There was something about him—his rapid rise, his perfect record—that didn't sit right with her. It was too clean, too polished. And in her experience, people who seemed too good to be true usually were.

Rodriguez said "good night" to her partner and retreated to her room next door, the thunder roared overhead, a reminder of the turbulent world outside. But Lisa knew that the real storm would come tomorrow, in the courtroom of Jefferson Parish. And she and Enzo would be there, ready to see if Travis Hale was as untouchable as his reputation suggested—or if they had finally found the thread that would unravel the truth behind the murders.

With that thought, Lisa closed her eyes, the sound of the rain lulling her into a restless sleep. Tomorrow, they would confront Travis Hale. And one way or another, they would get the answers they needed.

CHAPTER SIXTEEN

The night was heavy with a damp, oppressive air. Daryl Jacobs stood in the shadows, his eyes narrowed, waiting for the right moment. He had spent the last few hours gathering a small group of men he knew he could count on—hard men, men who could handle themselves when things got rough. This wasn't the first time they had been up to no good, and Daryl knew it wouldn't be the last.

His anger simmered beneath the surface, waiting to erupt. The storm that had raged through the night had finally begun to ease, leaving the world eerily quiet in its wake. The rain-soaked earth squelched beneath their boots as they moved silently towards the trailer park, a remote spot often frequented by tourists looking for a taste of the swamp.

It was just after 4 AM when they arrived. The trailer they were looking for sat on the edge of the park, barely visible in the dim light. Inside where the two men Daryl was certain were responsible for his brother's murder—two outsiders, two Black men who had crossed the wrong person. Daryl's heart pounded in his chest, each beat echoing the fury he felt. They were going to pay.

He gave the signal, and one of his men—a tall, wiry guy named Ray—stepped forward, a bottle in his hand, its ragged top already aflame. Ray hurled it through a window, and the glass shattered with a piercing scream. The night lit up as fire licked at the edges of the curtains, the orange glow casting wild shadows against the trees.

Inside the trailer, there was chaos. Shouts of panic rang out, followed by the sound of a door being thrown open in desperation. The two men bolted outside, their eyes wide with fear, but they didn't get far. Daryl's mob descended on them like wolves on prey, fists and feet flying in a blur of violence.

They fought back as best they could, but they were outnumbered and overwhelmed. Daryl swung a heavy fist, catching one of them in the mouth. Blood sprayed, mingling with the mud beneath them. The other man was on the ground, curled into a ball, trying to protect his head as the kicks rained down. The night was filled with the sound of grunts, the dull thud of fists meeting flesh, and the wet splatter of blood on the earth.

It was brutal, savage. The kind of beating that left nothing but broken bodies and a sense of hollow satisfaction. Daryl watched, his chest heaving, as the life drained from their eyes. This wasn't justice—this was revenge. And as the sun began to creep over the horizon, the first light of day revealed the horror of what they had done.

CHAPTER SEVENTEEN

Sheriff Landry arrived at the trailer park just as the first rays of dawn were breaking over the horizon. The scene was grim. Two bodies, broken and barely clinging to life, were being carefully loaded into ambulances. The medics worked quickly but gently; their faces set in expressions of grim determination.

Landry's young deputy, Mike Harris, barely out of the academy, approached him with a clipboard in hand. The boy's eyes were wide, the shock of the night's violence still fresh. "Sheriff," he began, his voice steady despite the obvious horror of what he had just witnessed, "we've got eyewitness testimony from a few residents who saw the whole thing. They gave good descriptions of the men involved, including Daryl Jacobs."

The sheriff nodded, his face a mask of controlled anger. He had warned Daryl. Told him to leave things alone, to let the law handle it. But Daryl, hot-headed and vengeful, hadn't listened. And now, two men lay at death's door because of it.

Within hours, Daryl and his buddies had been rounded up. Daryl sat now in a small, cold interrogation room, directly across from Landry. The sheriff looked at him with a mixture of anger and something close to pity. "You're going away for a few years, Daryl," he said, his voice flat. "I told you not to take the law into your own hands. Those two guys you and your friends beat to a pulp—they were just looking for jobs. Olivia's mother had offered them some work."

Daryl shifted uncomfortably in his seat, his bravado faltering under the weight of Landry's gaze. "But my brother…" he started, but Landry cut him off, leaning forward, his voice low and filled with barely restrained fury.

"Your brother's murder has taken a new direction, Daryl. He's a victim of a serial killer that the FBI is now investigating." The words hung in the air, heavy and final. Daryl's eyes widened in shock, the reality of his situation sinking in. He had attacked innocent men, fuelled by nothing but anger and grief. And now, the truth was so much worse than he had imagined.

Landry stood up, the disgust evident in his eyes as he looked down at Daryl. "Take him away," he ordered his officers, his voice laced with disappointment. As they led Daryl out of the room, the sheriff remained behind, his mind already turning to the bigger issue at hand—the hunt for the real killer. The trailer park, the beating, Daryl Jacobs—all of it seemed small in comparison to the darkness that was now creeping into their town.

CHAPTER EIGHTEEN

Agents Rodriguez and Romano exited their unmarked sedan in front of the Jefferson Parish County Courthouse, a looming structure of limestone and glass that seemed to tower over the surrounding buildings. The courthouse stood like a fortress, a bastion of law and order where justice was dispensed with cold, calculated precision. They were here to witness the man everyone in law enforcement called "the number one DOA," Travis Hale, in his element.

The two agents had heard plenty about Hale—his reputation preceded him in every corner of the legal system. Hale was the kind of prosecutor who didn't just win cases; he obliterated his opponents, turning what seemed like tenuous charges into irrefutable truths in the minds of the jury. Today, he was prosecuting a nineteen-year-old white male, accused of robbing a post office at gunpoint—a crime that could very well ruin the young man's life if convicted.

Inside, the courtroom buzzed with quiet anticipation. The gallery was full, packed with observers who had come to see Hale work his magic. Rodrigues and Romano found seats near the back, just in time to catch the beginning of Hale's closing argument. They exchanged a brief, knowing glance—this was the moment they'd been waiting for.

Travis Hale stood tall and composed at the prosecution's table, his presence radiating a calm authority that commanded the room's attention. He was in his late forties, with sharp features and a measured gaze that never seemed to miss a detail. He didn't rely on theatrics or raised voices; his power came from the simplicity and clarity of his words. Every gesture was deliberate, every pause calculated. It was as if the courtroom itself bent to his will.

"Ladies and gentlemen of the jury," Hale began, his voice steady and smooth, "let's talk about what we know."

He walked toward the jury box, his gaze sweeping across the faces of the jurors, holding each one for just a beat longer than necessary. The room seemed to tighten around him as he spoke, as if everyone was leaning in, hanging on his every word.

"The defendant, a young man, just nineteen years old, was found in possession of a shotgun that matches the description of the weapon used in the robbery. He was seen leaving the vicinity of the post office not long after the crime was committed. And while his mother has given him an alibi, let's be honest—what mother wouldn't want to protect her son?"

Hale paused, allowing the gravity of his words to sink in. The courtroom was utterly silent.

"We also have the victim, a postal worker who was terrified for her life, describing a man who fits the defendant's height and build. Sure, some of the evidence may be circumstantial, but taken together, it paints a very clear picture."

Rodriguez watched as the jury members nodded almost imperceptibly. Hale was getting inside their heads, guiding them toward the conclusion he wanted them to reach.

"Now, the defence would have you believe that the defendant is just an innocent kid who happened to be in the wrong place at the wrong time," Hale continued, his tone sharpening just slightly. "But the truth is, ladies and gentlemen, the defendant made choices. He chose to arm himself. He chose to rob that post office. And now, he must face the consequences of those choices."

Hale turned, pacing slowly in front of the jury, letting his words settle in the air. He wasn't just speaking to their minds—he was speaking to their sense of duty, to their belief in justice.

"You've seen the evidence, you've heard the testimony, and deep down, you know the truth. This isn't about ruining a young man's life; it's about protecting our community. It's about sending a message that we will not tolerate this kind of violence, no matter who commits it."

He stopped, turning to face the jury directly, his eyes locked onto theirs. "The evidence points to one undeniable fact: the defendant is guilty."

As Hale returned to his seat, the air in the courtroom felt charged, as if an invisible thread connected him to the jury. Romano leaned in to whisper to Rodriguez, "He's got them eating out of his hand."

Rodriguez nodded, still watching Hale with a mix of awe and caution. "He's dangerous, no doubt about it."

Three hours later, the jury returned with a verdict— guilty on all counts. The young man's face went pale as the reality of his situation set in. Hale remained composed, accepting the verdict with the same calm demeanour he'd maintained throughout the trial.

As the courtroom began to empty, Rodriguez and Romano lingered for a moment, taking in the scene. Hale had done it again. He'd taken a case with more than its share of holes and sewn it up so tightly that the jury hadn't hesitated in their decision.

"I almost feel sorry for the kid," Romano muttered as they walked out of the courtroom.

"Almost," Rodriguez agreed. "But Hale... he's something else. We'll need to keep an eye on him."

"Definitely," Romano said. "He's not just a prosecutor—he's a force of nature."

As they stepped outside into the bright afternoon sun, the agents knew they'd just witnessed something powerful, something that would stay with them long after the echoes of the gavel had faded. Travis Hale wasn't just a prosecutor—he was a man who could bend the truth to his will and make it dance in the minds of those who mattered most. And that made him the most dangerous kind of adversary.

CHAPTER NINETEEN

Agents Rodriguez and Romano stood at the base of the courthouse steps, the Louisiana sun casting long shadows as the late afternoon began to cool. The crowd that had gathered for the high-profile trial was dispersing, leaving behind only a few stragglers—journalists scribbling last-minute notes, spectators chatting about the outcome, and the occasional law enforcement officer keeping a watchful eye on the scene.

The two agents had one last task before they could consider their day done: a conversation with the man of the hour, District Attorney Travis Hale. The guilty verdict had been delivered just hours ago, and the courtroom had since emptied. But as the courthouse doors swung open, Rodriguez and Romano straightened, their eyes locking onto Hale as he emerged.

Hale appeared as composed as ever, his dark suit still immaculate, his expression calm and collected. Beside him was his shadow, the infamous Crazy Dog Kowalski, a burly man with a face weathered by years on the police force. Kowalski's eyes darted around the courtyard, always vigilant, while Hale exuded an air of untouchable confidence.

Rodriguez and Romano approached them with purpose. "Congratulations on the verdict, Mr. Hale," Rodriguez said, extending a hand.

Hale paused, glancing at Rodriguez's hand before taking it with a brief, perfunctory shake. "Thank you," he replied, his tone courteous but distant.

Romano stepped forward, flashing his FBI badge with a practised flick of his wrist. "Agents Rodriguez and Romano, FBI. We'd like a word with you, Mr. Hale."

For a split second, something flickered in Hale's eyes—annoyance, perhaps, or disdain—but it was gone as quickly as it appeared. He didn't bother to hide his irritation, a slight curl at the corner of his mouth betraying his thoughts.

"I'm afraid I'm quite busy," Hale said coolly, withdrawing his hand and nodding toward the courthouse. "If you'd like to speak with me, you can contact my secretary and schedule an appointment."

Rodrigues wasn't about to be brushed off so easily. "This won't take long, Mr. Hale. It's about some of the cases you've lost, we've noticed—"

Hale cut him off with a dismissive wave. "Agents, I understand that you have your job to do, but so do I. Now, if you'll excuse me, I have other matters to attend to."

Kowalski, who had been silent up until now, stepped closer to Hale, his imposing frame casting a long shadow over the two agents. He didn't say a word, but his presence alone was enough to signal that the conversation was over.

Rodriguez and Romano exchanged a quick glance, both recognizing the futility of pushing further at that moment. "We'll be in touch," Romano said, his voice steady, though there was a hard edge to it.

"Looking forward to it," Hale replied with a tight smile, though it didn't reach his eyes.

Without another word, Hale turned on his heel, and Kowalski followed closely behind. The two men descended the courthouse steps and headed toward a sleek, black car idling at the curb. The driver, a nondescript man in dark sunglasses, held the door open for Hale, who slid into the back seat with a proficient ease. Kowalski followed, shutting the door behind them with a solid thud.

As the car pulled away, Kowalski broke the silence inside the vehicle. "Congratulations, boss," he said, his voice gruff, but with a hint of admiration.

Hale didn't immediately respond. He was still replaying the interaction with the FBI agents in his mind, considering what it might mean. Finally, he nodded, a knowing grin spreading across his face. "Thank you, Kowalski. Another one in the bag."

Kowalski chuckled, a low, rumbling sound. He had been Hale's right-hand man for years, and he knew the DA better than anyone. Hale's confidence was well-earned; after all, they were an unstoppable team. Kowalski's role as an investigator was more than just gathering facts and evidence—he was the enforcer, the one who made sure the details lined up exactly as they needed to.

As the car sped through the streets of Jefferson Parish, Kowalski's mind wandered to the work he had put in for this case. He had spent countless hours re-checking crime scenes, interviewing witnesses, and securing files that weren't exactly within his reach. His connections in the underbelly of the city—petty criminals, drug addicts, and other lowlifes—had fed him information that he used to piece together the narrative Hale needed. It wasn't always by the book, and sometimes it meant skirting the edges of the law, but Kowalski didn't mind. The results spoke for themselves.

"Those FBI agents, you think they'll be a problem?" Kowalski asked, breaking the silence.

Hale considered the question for a moment. "They might be persistent, but they won't find anything. We're too careful about that."

"Yeah," Kowalski agreed. "Nothing left undone."

Hale's smile widened as he looked out the window, the city streets blurring past. "That's right, Crazy Dog. Nothing left undone."

In the rearview mirror, the driver caught Hale's eye and nodded. He had been with Hale and Kowalski long enough to know that when the DA said something, it was as good as law.

As the car sped on, leaving the courthouse—and the FBI agents—far behind, Hale allowed himself a moment of satisfaction. He and Kowalski were untouchable, a team that didn't just play to win; they played to dominate. And in their world, there was no room for mistakes, no second chances for those who stood in their way. Whether the defendants were guilty, or innocent didn't matter; what mattered was that Hale and Kowalski always came out on top.

And that, Hale thought, was how it would always be.

CHAPTER TWENTY

The night air in downtown New Orleans was electric, the streets pulsing with life as Travis Hale and Crazy Dog Kowalski made their way to their favourite bar. Nestled in the heart of the French Quarter, the bar was a well-kept secret among the city's elite—a place where deals were made, secrets were traded, and power was flaunted without shame. Tonight, it would be the stage for their victory celebration.

The bar's façade was unassuming, but once inside, the atmosphere was anything but. Rich, dark wood lined the walls, and the low lighting created an air of intimacy. The place was alive with the sound of jazz, the clink of glasses, and the murmur of conversations. It was a place where money spoke, and Hale and Kowalski's money talked loudly.

They strode in like they owned the place, which, in a way, they did. The bartender, a man who had seen it all, greeted them with a nod, already reaching for the top-shelf whisky that Hale favoured. The bar was packed, but as soon as Hale and Kowalski entered, a space seemed to open around them, as if the crowd instinctively knew to make way.

"Whisky, neat," Hale ordered, his voice carrying a tone of command. Kowalski followed suit, ordering the same.

The drinks were poured swiftly, the amber liquid glinting in the low light. Hale raised his glass, his eyes locking with Kowalski's. "To another win," he said, his voice full of quiet satisfaction.

Kowalski clinked his glass against Hale's. "To us," he replied with a grin, before downing the whisky in one smooth motion.

The night was theirs, and the drinks began to flow freely. As the hours passed, the bar filled even more, word of Hale's courtroom triumph spreading quickly. Pretty women, drawn to their aura of power and confidence, gravitated toward them. Hale, ever the charmer, handled them with the same finesse he used in the courtroom—smooth, assured, and always in control. Kowalski, rougher around the edges, had his own appeal—a raw, dangerous energy that intrigued just as much as it intimidated.

At one point, a beautiful brunette with striking green eyes leaned in close to Hale, her laughter ringing out as he whispered something in her ear. She was all smiles, clearly enamoured by the DA's charisma. Meanwhile, Kowalski found himself with a fiery redhead who seemed more than eager to match his intensity.

The night wore on, the jazz was playing on, and the drinks kept coming. Hale didn't care about the cost; he was flush with the thrill of victory, and tonight, money was no object. The women were the perfect icing on the cake—a reward for a job well done.

As the bar began to thin out, the atmosphere shifting from lively to intimate, Hale knew it was time to make his move. He downed the last of his whisky, the burn a pleasant reminder of the night's success, and turned to the brunette who had been by his side most of the evening. "How about we take this party somewhere a little more private?" he suggested, his voice low and inviting.

She smiled, her eyes glittering with interest. "Lead the way."

Kowalski, overhearing, exchanged a look with the redhead who had been practically draped over him all night. "Sounds like a plan," he said, rising from his seat with the woman on his arm.

They left the bar together, Hale and Kowalski each with a woman by their side. The night air was cool, a refreshing contrast to the warmth of the bar. They walked through the vibrant streets of the French Quarter, the sounds of the city fading behind them as they made their way to Hale's car—a sleek black sedan waiting just a block away.

The drive to Hale's apartment was quick, the streets quieting as they left the bustling heart of the city. Hale's apartment was a modern, luxurious penthouse in an upscale neighbourhood overlooking the beach. The building was one of the most exclusive in New Orleans, a testament to Hale's success and his taste for the finer things in life.

They arrived at the building, and the doorman nodded to Hale as he led the group inside. The elevator ride was silent, the anticipation thick in the air. When they reached the top floor, the doors opened directly into Hale's apartment, revealing a space that was as impressive as it was opulent.

The living room was expansive, with floor-to-ceiling windows offering a breathtaking view of the moonlit beach below. The décor was sleek and modern, with dark leather furniture, polished wood floors, and a large fireplace that added a touch of warmth to the otherwise minimalist space. Art pieces—carefully selected and undoubtedly expensive—adorned the walls, adding splashes of colour to the monochromatic palette.

"Make yourselves at home," Hale said, his voice smooth as he gestured to the room. He poured them all drinks from the well-stocked bar in the corner, handing each woman a glass before raising his own. "To new friends," he toasted.

They drank, and the atmosphere quickly turned from celebratory to intimate. The women, already drawn to Hale and Kowalski's magnetic presence, were now completely captivated. They moved from the living room to the expansive balcony, where the sound of the waves crashing against the shore added a calming background to the night.

The stars above reflected in the dark ocean, and for a moment, Hale stood at the edge of the balcony, looking out over the water. The success of the day, the power he held, the beautiful woman by his side—it was all exactly as it should be. He had worked hard to get here, to be the man who could sway a jury, who could command a room, who could live a life of luxury and excess. And he had no intention of letting anything or anyone take it away from him.

Behind him, Kowalski and the redhead were laughing, the sound mingling with the crashing waves. The brunette slipped her arm around Hale's waist, leaning into him as she gazed out at the view.

"It's beautiful," she murmured, her voice filled with awe.

Hale turned to her, a confident smile on his face. "It is," he agreed, though his thoughts were far from the view. "But tonight, it's just the beginning."

As the night stretched into the early hours of the morning, the celebration continued in Hale's apartment. It was a night of indulgence, of excess, of power fully realised. For Hale and Kowalski, it was just another victory in a long line of triumphs—a night that would be remembered, not just for the courtroom success, but for the way they lived: on their terms, with no apologies, and with no regrets.

CHAPTER TWENTY-ONE

The sun was beginning to break through the clouds in the Louisiana sky, as the heat began to dry out the cobblestone streets of downtown New Orleans. The air was thick with the scent of magnolias and the distant notes of a jazz band playing somewhere near Jackson Square. FBI agents Enzo Romano and Lisa Rodriguez navigated the narrow streets in their black sedan, the humid air seeping through the windows despite the air conditioning.

The city was alive with its usual charm—an intoxicating blend of history, culture, and a hint of mystery. Enzo, with his neatly combed dark hair and sharp suit, drove in silence, his eyes scanning the streets, ever vigilant. Beside him, Lisa, her chestnut hair pulled into a tight bun, reviewed the case files on her tablet. She was a study in focus, her green eyes flickering with determination.

"Travis Hales' office should be just up ahead," Enzo said, breaking the silence.

Lisa nodded, glancing out the window at the passing storefronts and vibrant murals. "Let's see what he's got for us."

They pulled up in front of a modest, two-storey building that blended into the historical architecture of the area. The plaque by the entrance read: *Travis Hale Attorney*. The building was unassuming, with red brick walls and tall, narrow windows that allowed just enough light to spill inside without revealing too much to the outside world. A few plants in large terracotta pots flanked the entrance, and a simple brass knocker adorned the heavy wooden door.

Inside, the office was a world of its own—quiet, orderly, and efficient, much like the man they were about to meet. The walls were lined with dark wood panelling, and the air was cool, a welcome contrast to the oppressive heat outside. The scent of polished wood and fresh coffee filled the space, mingling with the faint aroma of something sweet.

As they stepped into the reception area, they were greeted by Mrs. Smith, Travis Hales' long-time secretary. A woman in her fifties with sharp eyes and black hair styled into a neat bob, Mrs. Smith was the kind of person who commanded respect without uttering a word. She had been with Travis since the beginning, ten years ago, when Hales Consulting Group was nothing more than an idea. Over the years, she had become the backbone of the office, handling everything from scheduling to making lunch for Travis, treating him more like a son than a boss.

"Good morning," Mrs. Smith greeted them, her voice warm but brisk. Her sharp gaze softened slightly as she took in the sight of the two agents. "You must be Agents Romano and Rodriguez. Mr. Hale is expecting you."

"Thank you," Enzo replied, his tone respectful.

Mrs. Smith nodded, rising from her desk. The office around her was immaculate, with a large, vintage clock ticking softly on the wall and a few framed photographs of New Orleans landmarks decorating the space. A bouquet of fresh flowers sat in a vase on her desk, adding a touch of colour to the otherwise subdued environment.

"This way, please," she said, leading them down a short hallway.

As they walked, Enzo noticed the subtle signs of Mrs. Smith's meticulous care—everything in its place, no clutter, no chaos. She moved with the efficiency of someone who knew her job inside out, but there was a quiet sadness about her, something that only those who looked closely would see. Lisa, ever observant, picked up on it immediately. She had read in her research that Mrs. Smith's husband had recently been diagnosed with Alzheimer's, and she knew the woman was close to leaving the job she had held so dearly for so many years.

Mrs. Smith stopped in front of a heavy wooden door and knocked softly before opening it. "Mr. Hale, the agents are here."

"Thank you, Mrs. Smith. Please, come in," came the reply from inside.

She opened the door wider, allowing Enzo and Lisa to step inside before she closed it quietly behind them.

Travis Hale rose from behind his large mahogany desk, a friendly smile on his face. He was a man in his late forties, with dark hair just beginning to show streaks of grey at the temples. His suit was impeccably tailored, and his demeanour was one of calm confidence. The office reflected his personality—tasteful, understated, but with an air of authority. The walls were adorned with framed diplomas, certificates, and a few pieces of abstract art that added a splash of colour to the otherwise muted tones of the room.

"Agents Romano, Rodriguez, welcome," Travis said, extending a hand first to Enzo and then to Lisa. His handshake was firm, his gaze direct but not intimidating. Far different from the dismissive attitude they encountered at the courthouse.

"Thank you for seeing us on such short notice, Mr. Hale," Enzo replied, taking a seat as Travis gestured toward the two chairs in front of his desk.

"Not at all. I'm happy to help in any way I can," Travis said, taking his seat again. "Can I offer you some coffee? Mrs. Smith makes an excellent brew. We also have some of her homemade king cake if you're interested."

Lisa smiled politely. "Coffee would be great, thank you."

Travis pressed a button on his desk phone. "Mrs. Smith, could you bring in some coffee for our guests?"

"Of course, Mr. Hale," came the efficient reply.

As they waited, Travis leaned back slightly in his chair, studying the two agents. "I understand you're here about the recent developments in the John Jacobs case?"

Enzo nodded, leaning forward slightly. "Yes. We're hoping you might be able to shed some light on a few things."

Travis's expression grew serious, the friendly smile fading into something more reserved. "I'll do what I can, Agent Romano. But as you know, discretion is key in my line of work. I'll need to know exactly what you're looking for."

Before Enzo could respond, Mrs. Smith re-entered the room, carrying a tray with three steaming mugs of coffee and a plate of colourful slices of king cake, each piece decorated with the traditional purple, green, and gold sugar. She set the tray down on the coffee table in front of the agents and Travis, her movements as precise and graceful as always.

"Thank you, Mrs. Smith," Travis said, his tone warm. "That will be all for now."

Mrs. Smith gave a small nod, her eyes lingering on Travis for a moment, a silent exchange that spoke volumes about the years they had worked together. Then, she turned and left the room, closing the door softly behind her.

Enzo took a sip of the coffee, appreciating the rich, robust flavour. "This is excellent, Mr. Hale. You're lucky to have someone like Mrs. Smith."

Travis smiled, a hint of sadness in his eyes. "I know. She's one of a kind. I don't know what I'll do when she leaves."

Lisa glanced at Enzo, then back at Travis. "It's clear you run a tight ship here, Mr. Hales. That's part of why we're here. We need someone with your… attention to detail to help us connect some dots."

Travis set his coffee cup down, folding his hands on the desk. "I see. Well, Agents, let's get to it then. Tell me what you need to know."

As they began to discuss the five cases, the quiet hum of the office outside the door seemed to fade into the background. Travis Hale, with his calm demeanour and sharp mind, was about to become an integral part of their investigation. And as Enzo and Lisa delved deeper into their conversation with him, they couldn't help but wonder just how much more the man behind the desk knew—and how much he was willing to share.

CHAPTER TWENTY-TWO

The atmosphere in Travis Hales' office had shifted. What began as a cordial meeting had become something more intense, charged with an undercurrent of suspicion. Enzo Romano and Lisa Rodriguez exchanged a brief glance, silently communicating their readiness for what was about to unfold.

Travis Hale, seated behind his imposing mahogany desk, noticed the change, too. His fingers drummed lightly on the polished wood as he observed the two agents. His demeanour was still composed, but there was a slight tension in his posture, a tightening around his eyes. The silence that had settled in the room was almost palpable, broken only by the soft ticking of the vintage clock on the wall.

Enzo leaned forward, his elbows resting on the edge of the desk. His voice was calm but laced with the weight of the questions he was about to ask. "Mr. Hale, we appreciate your cooperation so far. But there's something we need to discuss in more detail. It's about the cases you've lost over the past few years."

Travis raised an eyebrow, a flicker of confusion crossing his face. "My losses? What about them?"

Lisa, who had been quietly observing, spoke up. "Each of those cases ended in acquittal. And in every instance, the defendants were found murdered shortly after, their head decapitated."

A shadow passed over Travis's face. He leaned back in his chair, folding his arms. "I'm aware of the tragedies that occurred. But I don't see what that has to do with me."

Enzo's gaze didn't waver. "We're trying to determine if there's a pattern here. Something we might have missed. Did you notice anything unusual during those trials? Perhaps something off about the juries? Could they have been bribed or influenced in some way?"

Travis's eyes narrowed, and he shook his head slowly. "Nothing like that. I was too focused on the cases themselves, as usual, to the best of my ability. I trust in the system and accept the verdict. If there had been any tampering, I would have noticed."

Lisa leaned in, her voice soft but probing. "What about the courtroom? Did you notice anyone who seemed out of place? Someone attending each trial, watching?"

Travis sighed, rubbing his temples as if trying to summon memories long buried beneath the stress of those high-profile cases. "I can't say I did. Courtrooms are usually filled with people, family members, journalists, and curious onlookers. I was too engrossed in the trials to keep track of who was sitting in the gallery."

There was a pause, the room thick with the weight of unspoken thoughts. Lisa's eyes were sharp, trained on Travis, while Enzo continued to watch him with a measured intensity.

Travis shifted uncomfortably, sensing the direction this interrogation was heading. His voice took on a defensive edge. "Are you suggesting that I had something to do with these murders?"

Enzo didn't flinch. "We're not suggesting anything, Mr. Hale. We're simply exploring every possibility."

Travis's expression hardened. "I'm a prosecution attorney. My job is to represent the state. I do my job, and I do it well."

Lisa nodded slowly, her tone conciliatory but firm. "We're not accusing you, Mr. Hale. But we must ask these questions. It's our job to consider every angle, every possibility. If there's something you know, something you might not have realised was important at the time, now's the time to tell us."

Travis's eyes flicked between the two agents, searching for any sign that they might be trying to trap him, to implicate him in something. But all he saw were two professionals doing their job, albeit with a level of scrutiny that made him uncomfortable.

"I've told you everything I know," Travis said, his voice steady but with a hint of frustration. "If there were any irregularities, they slipped past me. I was focused on the defendant, not looking for some conspiracy."

The room fell silent again, the ticking of the clock the only sound. Enzo and Lisa exchanged another glance, this time one of subtle frustration. They had hoped for more, something that might point them in a new direction. But Travis was either telling the truth or was an expert at concealing his involvement, if there was any at all.

After a moment, Enzo leaned back in his chair, his posture relaxing slightly. "We appreciate your time, Mr. Hale. We may need to speak with you again as the investigation continues."

Travis nodded, the tension easing from his shoulders. "Of course. I'll help however I can. But let me be clear—these murders, they horrify me, and I swear to you, I had no part in them."

Lisa gave a small, polite smile. "We understand, Mr. Hale. Thank you for your cooperation."

As they rose to leave, Travis remained seated, his gaze following them to the door. Mrs. Smith was waiting just outside, her expression as unreadable as ever. She nodded to the agents as they stepped into the hallway, her presence a reminder of the steady, controlled environment that Travis had built around himself.

Once outside the office, Enzo and Lisa walked in silence down the hallway, their footsteps echoing off the walls. They exited the building, the humid New Orleans air hitting them like a wall. Enzo took a deep breath, letting the heat wash over him.

"What do you think?" Lisa asked quietly as they walked toward their car.

Enzo didn't answer immediately. He was replaying the conversation in his mind, analysing every word, every gesture. "I think Hale is hiding something. Whether it's about the murders or something else, I don't know. But he's too smart not to have noticed anything unusual."

Lisa nodded, her own thoughts mirroring Enzo's. "We don't have anything concrete. Just a feeling."

"A sense of unease," Enzo agreed. "But no proof."

They reached the car, and Enzo unlocked it, pausing before getting in. "We'll have to keep digging. There's something more to this, I can feel it."

Lisa glanced back at the building, at the window that probably looked into Travis's office. "Yeah. But for now, we're running on instinct. Let's hope it's enough to lead us to the truth."

CHAPTER TWENTY-THREE

Travis Hale was sitting at his desk. It had been a couple of days since he'd last heard from the District Attorney's office, and though he tried to focus on the work at hand, a lingering tension gnawed at him. He knew that the wheels of justice moved slowly, but he couldn't shake the feeling that something significant was on the horizon.

The call he was waiting for, Mrs Smith put it through, "Rene Marshall." "Mr. Hale?" The voice on the other end was firm and professional, but not without a hint of empathy.

"Yes, speaking," Travis replied, gripping the phone a little tighter.

"This is Assistant District Attorney Renee Marshall. I'm calling to inform you that we've decided to move forward with the prosecution of Daryl Jacobs. We're charging him with two counts of attempted murder."

Travis felt a rush of emotions—relief, anger, and a sense of grim satisfaction that justice was finally within reach. "When?" he asked, his voice steadier than he expected.

"We're sending over the details of the charges. The preliminary hearing is scheduled to be held in Houma

County Court this coming Monday. At that time, we'll formally present the charges, and the defence will enter their plea. After the plea, the next step is jury selection," ADA Marshall explained. "The defence has already indicated they'll plead not guilty, so we'll proceed to trial. Given the seriousness of the charges, we expect the process to move quickly. A trial date has tentatively been set for three weeks from the hearing."

Travis leaned back in his chair, letting the information sink in. Three weeks. It wasn't long, but it was enough time for everything to change for better or worse.

"Thank you for letting me know," he said, his voice a mix of gratitude and resolve. "I'll be ready."

The ADA's tone softened slightly. "I understand this is a lot to process, Mr. Hale. But we're committed to seeing justice served. If you have any questions or need anything as we move forward, don't hesitate to reach out."

Travis nodded, even though she couldn't see him. "I appreciate that. I'll be in touch if I need anything."

They exchanged a few more words before the call ended. Travis sat there for a moment, phone still in hand. Daryl Jacobs was going to face the consequences of his actions.

The following Monday, Houma County Court was busier than usual. The courtroom buzzed with murmured conversations, the anticipation palpable as people filed in, waiting for the preliminary hearing to begin. Travis arrived early, accompanied by his investigator, 'crazy dog' Kowalski.

They took their seats near the front, Travis's eyes scanning the room until they settled on Daryl Jacobs, seated at the defence table. Jacobs looked smaller than Travis anticipated, his face drawn and pale.

The judge, an imposing figure with a stern expression, entered the courtroom, and the room fell silent. After the formalities, the charges were read out: one count of arson, two counts of attempted murder. The gravity of the words hung heavy in the air, a stark reminder of the seriousness of the accusations.

Jacobs's defence attorney, a slick-looking man with a silver tongue, rose to enter the plea. "Not guilty, Your Honor," he declared, his voice smooth and confident.

Travis's stomach churned at the words, though he had expected nothing less. This was only the beginning. The judge acknowledged the plea and swiftly moved the proceedings forward.

"We will now proceed to jury selection," the judge announced.

The process was meticulous, each potential juror was questioned and scrutinized by both the prosecution and the defence. It was a delicate dance, both sides looking for any sign of bias, any indication that a juror might lean too far one way or the other. Hours passed, and the atmosphere grew more tense with each passing minute. By the end of the day, twelve jurors were chosen—a diverse group of men and women who would ultimately decide Jacobs's fate.

As the hearing concluded, the judge set the trial date for three weeks later. The gavel struck with a definitive thud, signalling the end of the day's proceedings.

Outside the courthouse, Travis stood on the steps, the warm sun contrasting sharply with the cold knot of anxiety in his chest. Kowalski joined him, his expression unreadable.

"It's going to be a tough trial, Travis," Kowalski said, not one to sugarcoat the truth. "The defence is going to fight hard, but so are we."

Travis nodded, his jaw set in determination. "I'm ready for whatever comes next. I have to be, need you in the office tomorrow. We'll put together what you have to do."

With that, they parted ways, each preparing for the battle ahead in their own way. The clock was ticking, and in three weeks, they would all be back in that courtroom, ready to see justice done.

CHAPTER TWENTY-FOUR

Kowalski arrived at Travis Hale's office precisely at 8 a.m. sharp, as he had done countless times before. The small office building was still quiet, the only sound the faint hum of the cleaning crew finishing their morning rounds. Mrs. Smith, usually had coffee brewing by now, but Kowalski wasn't in the mood to wait. He strode past her empty desk and went straight to Travis's door.

Without bothering to knock, Kowalski pushed the door open and stepped inside. Travis looked up from a stack of papers, a hint of surprise on his face, but before he could say anything, Kowalski flopped down in the worn leather chair opposite the desk. He stretched out his legs, leaning back as if he owned the place.

"Okay, boss, what you got for me?" Kowalski drawled, crossing his arms behind his head.

Travis set down his pen and leaned forward, his expression serious. He had always valued Kowalski's no-nonsense approach, and today was no different. "This trial's going to be as tight as it could get, Kowalski. I need you to lock down everything. No loose ends."

Kowalski's eyes narrowed slightly, his attention fully on Travis now. "What do you need?"

"First, I need you to track down the eyewitness who saw Daryl at the scene. We need them to testify in court, no exceptions." Travis's voice was steady, but the urgency was clear.

"Got it. I'll find them," Kowalski replied, making a mental note. He was good at finding people, especially when they didn't want to be found.

"Next, I need you to go see Sheriff Landry. He warned Daryl not to take the law into his own hands, and we need him on the stand to testify to that. Landry's testimony could be crucial."

Kowalski nodded. He had a decent relationship with the sheriff, having worked with him on a few cases over the years. Getting Landry to testify shouldn't be too difficult, but Kowalski knew better than to assume anything.

"I'll handle it," Kowalski assured him.

"There's more," Travis continued, leaning back in his chair. "I need you to dig into Daryl's past. See if he's been involved in anything like this before—anything that could show a pattern of behaviour. We need to paint a full picture for the jury."

Kowalski grunted in acknowledgement. Daryl Jacobs wasn't exactly an open book, but Kowalski had ways of finding information that most people preferred to keep buried.

Travis hesitated for a moment, then continued, his voice a touch quieter. "I also need you to visit the hospital where the two men were taken after the attack. Get their records, Kowalski. We need to show how badly they were beaten, that they were practically on the edge of death. It's crucial to establish the severity of what Daryl did."

Kowalski's eyes darkened. He wasn't a fan of hospitals, but he knew this was a key part of the case. "I'll get the records," he said, his tone leaving no room for doubt.

"And one last thing," Travis added, almost as an afterthought. "Juror number three—I thought I saw a far-right tattoo on his arm. I need you to check him out, see if he has any connections we should be worried about. We can't afford any surprises during the trial."

Kowalski raised an eyebrow. "You want me to dig into a juror? That's risky business."

"I know," Travis admitted. "But we can't take any chances. If there's something there, we need to know about it. Quietly."

Kowalski didn't respond right away, mulling it over. It wasn't the first time he'd been asked to do something on the edge of legal, but it was the first time it involved a juror. After a moment, he gave a slow nod. "Alright, boss. I'll see what I can find."

Travis exhaled, some of the tension easing from his shoulders. "I appreciate it, Kowalski. We're going up against a tough defence, and we need every piece of evidence we can get."

Kowalski stood up, stretching his arms and rolling his neck. "I'll get started right away. You just keep the heat on Jacobs in court, and I'll handle the rest."

Travis watched as Kowalski headed for the door, already mentally ticking off the tasks he'd just been given. "And Kowalski," Travis called out, just as the ex-detective reached for the door handle.

"Yeah?" Kowalski turned back; one eyebrow raised.

"Be careful out there. This case is going to bring out the worst in some people."

Kowalski flashed a crooked grin. "Aren't you worried about them?"

Travis allowed himself a small smile. "Just get it done."

With a nod, Kowalski was gone, leaving Travis alone with his thoughts and the growing weight of the trial that loomed ahead. There was a lot riding on this case, and as

Travis sat back down at his desk, he knew that every move from here on out would be crucial. The trial was just weeks away, and there was no room for error.

In the hallway, Kowalski moved with purpose, already forming a plan in his mind. He had a lot to do and not much time to do it. But that was how he liked it. When the stakes were high, Kowalski was at his best. And this time, the stakes couldn't be higher.

CHAPTER TWENTY-FIVE

The clatter of utensils and the hum of casual conversation filled the cozy atmosphere of Maggie's Diner. The aroma of freshly brewed coffee mixed with the scent of sizzling bacon and eggs, creating a comforting, almost nostalgic feel. Agents Romano and Rodriguez sat in their usual booth near the back, where they had a clear view of the entrance and a partial view of the street outside. It was a strategic spot, perfect for watching and waiting, which is exactly what they had been doing for the past hour.

The case had gone cold. They had followed every lead, interrogated every possible witness, and still, they were no closer to solving it. Travis Hale, the man they had pinned their hopes on, had been a dead end. After A Day of relentless questioning, they got nothing more than vague statements and a lot of dodging. Hale was smart— too smart. He had a knack for walking the fine line between the legal and illegal, never fully crossing into territory that could get him locked up. They needed someone who could give them more, someone on the inside. That's when they turned their attention to Tony Kowalski.

Kowalski was a legend in law enforcement, having served thirty years on the police force. He'd worked his way up to detective, earning the nickname "The Headmaster" for his stern yet effective way of mentoring younger officers. Kowalski didn't just teach; he moulded. He was old school, the type who didn't always follow the rules but got the job done. He'd been known to bend the law when necessary, using his own brand of justice to keep the streets clean. After retiring from the force, he spent a few years as a private investigator, where his reputation continued to grow. Eventually, he landed a job as Travis Hale's personal investigator on prosecution cases.

The agents had done their homework. Kowalski's file was thick, filled with commendations, complaints, and everything in between. His methods were controversial, but his results were undeniable. He was the kind of man who had seen and done it all, and who, despite his age, still had a commanding presence that demanded respect. Kowalski was also fiercely loyal, which made him dangerous. If he was involved in this mess, it wasn't going to be easy to shake him down.

Romano glanced out the window, watching the cars pass by, his mind churning with possibilities. "You think Kowalski's dirty?" he asked, breaking the silence.

Rodriguez shrugged, finally settling down his fork. "Depends on what you mean by dirty. He's not clean, but that doesn't mean he's the bad guy. He's been around long enough to know how to cover his tracks. And he's got the reputation of someone who gets too close to the line."

Romano nodded, his gaze shifting back to his coffee. "Yeah, but close to the line and crossing it are two different things. We need to figure out which side he's on."

Rodriguez leaned back in the booth, crossing her arms. "He's been working with Hale for what, seven years now? That's a long time to build trust. If Hale's involved in something shady, Kowalski would know about it."

"That's what worries me," Romano said, his voice low. "If Kowalski's in on it, he's not just going to slip up and hand us what we need. We're going to have to watch him, see if he makes a mistake. Something small, something he doesn't even realize is a mistake."

Rodriguez nodded in agreement. "I've already put in for a surveillance team. We'll keep eyes on him around the clock, see who he meets, where he goes. Maybe he'll lead us to something or someone useful."

Romano took a sip of his coffee, his thoughts returning to their suspect. Tony Kowalski was a wild card, and they needed to play this carefully. The man was sharp, and if he got even a whiff that they were onto him, he'd shut down tighter than Hale. Patience was key. It was a waiting game now, and they had to be ready to strike when the moment came.

The door to the diner opened, the bell above it jingling softly. Both agents instinctively glanced up, but it was just a couple of locals coming in for breakfast. They relaxed back into their seats, but the tension remained.

"We'll get him," Rodriguez said quietly, more to herself than to Romano. "We'll get them both."

Romano didn't respond immediately. He simply stared into his coffee as if searching for answers in its dark depths. Finally, he looked up, his expression resolute. "Yeah, we will. It's just a matter of time."

The agents fell into a comfortable silence, the kind that comes from years of partnership and shared battles. Outside, the sun was starting to break through the morning clouds, casting a soft glow on the street. Inside Maggie's Diner, it was just another morning. But for Romano and Rodriguez, it was another step in the long, gruelling pursuit of justice. The waiting game had begun.

CHAPTER TWENTY-SIX

Tony Kowalski leaned back in his seat, tapping the steering wheel rhythmically as he watched the dilapidated trailer across the lot. The sun was dipping below the horizon, casting long shadows over the worn-out vehicles and rusted metal that dotted the trailer park. He had been there for hours, waiting patiently, as always. He was good at waiting; he had learned long ago that patience was as valuable as any weapon in his arsenal.

The door to the trailer finally creaked open, and a wiry man in his late fifties stepped out, squinting into the fading light. This was his guy, Earl Granger—a reclusive man with a reputation for minding his own business. But Granger had seen something, something that could change the course of the trial. Kowalski had spent days tracking him down, piecing together his whereabouts, and now he had him.

Kowalski opened the door to his car and stepped out, making his way over to Granger with the confident stride of someone who belonged. Granger looked up as Kowalski approached, his eyes narrowing in suspicion.

"Earl Granger?" Kowalski asked, though he already knew the answer.

"Who's askin'?" Granger replied, his voice rough and wary.

Kowalski pulled out his badge, not the official one he used back in his police days, but the one that said he was now a licensed private investigator. "Tony Kowalski. I'm here about the case involving Daryl Jacob."

Granger's expression hardened. "I don't want no trouble. I already told the cops what I saw."

"I know," Kowalski said, his tone calm and reassuring. "But it's not the cops who need to hear it. It's the jury. We need you to testify, Earl. What you saw could put Jacob away for good."

Granger hesitated, glancing around the empty lot as if expecting someone to jump out at him. "I ain't got no love for Jacob, but testifyin'… That's different. Folks around here, don't forget."

Kowalski leaned in closer, his voice lowering. "You've got a chance to do something right, Earl. Those two men deserve justice, and you're the one who can help give it to them. I'll make sure you're protected, and that nothing happens to you. But you must stand up and say what you saw."

Granger sighed, running a hand through his thinning hair. Finally, he nodded. "Alright. I'll do it. But you better keep your word, Kowalski."

"You have my word," Kowalski said, sealing the deal with a firm handshake. One witness down, two more to go.

The meeting with Sheriff Landry had gone as expected. The sheriff, a burly man with a stern demeanour, had known Kowalski for years. They had crossed paths more than once back in the day, and while Landry wasn't one to bend the law, he respected Kowalski's methods.

"So you're telling me you need me to testify?" Landry asked, leaning back in his chair in the cramped office of the sheriff's station.

"Just to confirm what you already know, Sheriff," Kowalski replied. "Your testimony will solidify the timeline and corroborate the other evidence. The jury needs to hear it from someone they trust."

Landry let out a long breath. "Alright, Kowalski. I'll do it."

Juror 3, however, was a different beast altogether.

The courthouse receptionist had been easy enough to bribe. A few thousand dollars had slipped into her pocket, and within a day, Kowalski had the address he needed. The house was out in the countryside, far from prying eyes. Kowalski had parked his car at a safe distance, using binoculars to observe the property. It didn't take long to get a sense of who he was dealing with. The Confederate flag flapped lazily in the breeze from the front porch, accompanied by religious symbols nailed to the weather-beaten siding of the house. A large, muscular Doberman patrolled the yard, growling at anyone who dared approach.

Kowalski watched for days, blending into the surroundings, careful not to attract attention. Juror 3 was a man of routine, which made him predictable. Every evening, just after sunset, he'd leave his house and drive a short distance to a small county hall. Kowalski followed him on the third night, keeping a safe distance as the juror's car pulled into the nearly deserted parking lot. The hall was unremarkable, the kind of place where community meetings or bingo nights would be held.

Kowalski entered the building cautiously, mingling at the back, staying in the shadows. The room was dimly lit, with a small group of men gathered around a podium. As they settled in, Kowalski's heart sank. The whispers, the hoods, the symbols—this wasn't just a meeting. It was a Klan gathering.

He kept his expression neutral, blending in with the other attendees, but inside, his mind was racing. This was dangerous territory, more dangerous than anything he'd anticipated. But he needed proof. If Juror 3 was attending

KKK meetings, it could mean a biased verdict in the trial, something that could swing the case in Jacob's favour.

Kowalski discreetly pulled out his phone, using it as a makeshift camera. He snapped photos whenever he could, careful not to draw attention. It was nerve-wracking work, but he was experienced enough to stay calm under pressure. He captured images of the juror, the others in the room, the Klan symbols, and anything else that might be useful.

After an hour, the meeting began to wind down. Kowalski slipped out before anyone could notice his absence, his heart still pounding. He got back to his car, the night air cool against his skin, and took a deep breath. He had what he needed: proof that Juror 3 was compromised.

As he drove away, Kowalski's mind raced with possibilities. The photos would be invaluable, but they also opened a new can of worms. He was playing with fire, and he knew it. If anyone found out what he had, it could end badly. But this was the line he walked, the thin line between justice and danger. And he'd walk it if he had to. There was no turning back now.

In the judge's chambers, the atmosphere was tense as Travis Hale, the lead prosecutor, presented damning evidence to the judge and the defence attorney. The photographs and information gathered by Tony

Kowalski, revealing Juror 3's involvement in a secret KKK meeting, were laid out on the table. Hale argued that the juror's presence at such a gathering was undeniable proof of bias, compromising the integrity of the trial. The defence attorney, visibly agitated, tried to downplay the significance of the evidence, but the judge's stern gaze made it clear where she stood. After reviewing the material, she ruled in favour of Hale's motion, ordering Juror 3's immediate removal from the case. A reserve juror was swiftly brought forward, ensuring the trial could proceed without the taint of prejudice.

CHAPTER TWENTY-SEVEN

The courthouse heaved with anticipation as the trial of Daryl Jacob began. The small town had never seen anything like it. The case had drawn national attention, and the gallery was packed with reporters, curious locals, and family members of the victims. The air was thick with tension, a mixture of expectation and dread.

Tony Kowalski sat next to his boss as usual, his eyes were fixed on the defendant, Daryl Jacob, who sat at the defence table with an air of smug confidence. Jacob was dressed in a crisp suit, his hair neatly combed back. To the untrained eye, he looked like any other man trying to clear his name.

Judge Mansfield, a stern woman with a reputation for no-nonsense rulings, called the court to order. The first witness was summoned, and the trial officially began.

The prosecution started strong, calling Dr Evelyn Marlowe to the stand. A seasoned physician with years of experience in trauma cases, Dr Marlowe exuded calm authority as she took the oath and settled into the witness chair. She was well-prepared, and as the prosecution began questioning her, it became clear why.

"Dr Marlowe, can you describe the injuries sustained by the victims in this case?" Travis asked, his tone measured and deliberate.

Dr Marlowe nodded, glancing briefly at the jurors before focusing on the prosecutor. "Both victims suffered extensive injuries consistent with a severe and prolonged beating. There were multiple fractures ribs, arms, and facial bones along with deep contusions and lacerations. The damage was extensive."

Travis Hale approached the evidence table and picked up a folder. "Your Honor, I'd like to submit these photographs and X-rays as evidence," he said, handing them to the bailiff, who then passed them to the judge.

"Proceed," the judge said, her voice echoing in the silent courtroom.

Travis held up a series of photographs, displaying them to the jury. The images were gruesome—close-ups of the victims' battered bodies, the X-rays showing broken bones in stark black and white.

"Dr Marlowe, can you walk us through these images?" Travis Hale asked.

Dr Marlowe obliged, detailing each injury with clinical precision. The jurors watched intently, some wincing at the severity of the injuries. As she spoke, the full horror of what had happened to those men became palpable in the room. The brutality was undeniable, and the evidence was damning.

When Travis finished, he glanced at the defence table. Jacob's attorney, a slick, silver-tongued man who had made a name for himself defending the indefensible, stood up to cross-examine.

"Dr Marlowe," he began, his tone smooth and confident, "is it possible that these injuries could have been sustained in an altercation with more than one attacker?"

Dr Marlowe didn't hesitate. "Yes, it's already been established it was more than one assailant, the pattern of injuries suggests a sustained assault by a group of individuals."

The defence attorney smiled, though it didn't reach his eyes. "So my client might not have taken part in this horrific attack at all?"

"Objection", Travis interjected.

"Sustained", the judge agreed. "How would Dr Marlowe know?"

The attorney nodded, seeming satisfied with her response. "No further questions."

Dr Marlowe stepped down, and Travis called the next witness: Sheriff Landry. The sheriff was a large man, with a presence that commanded respect. He took the oath, then sat down, adjusting his uniform slightly as he faced the prosecutor, Travis Hale.

"Sheriff Landry, can you tell the court about your interactions with the defendant, Daryl Jacob?" Travis asked.

Landry nodded; his expression serious. "Daryl Jacob is well-known around here. He runs a swamp tour business, but he's also got a reputation for handling things his own way when he feels the law isn't doing its job."

Travis Hale leaned in slightly. "What do you mean by that, Sheriff?"

Landry cleared his throat. "There was an incident a while back where Daryl implied that if the police didn't deal with certain individuals, he would take matters into his own hands."

There was a murmur in the courtroom, but the judge quickly silenced it with a sharp rap of her gavel.

"And what individuals was he referring to?" Travis pressed.

"The families involved with the John Jacobs acquittal," Landry said, his voice grave. "Daryl, the defendant thought they might have taken justice into their own hands".

Travis let the weight of Landry's words hang in the air before continuing. "In your professional opinion, Sheriff, do you believe Daryl Jacob was capable of carrying out such an act?"

Landry hesitated for a fraction of a second before answering. "Yes, I do."

The defence attorney jumped up, ready for his cross-examination. "Sheriff Landry, isn't it true that Daryl Jacob has always cooperated with law enforcement in the past?"

"Yes, he has," Landry admitted.

"And isn't it also true that Daryl Jacob has never been convicted of a violent crime?"

Landry nodded reluctantly. "That's correct."

The defence attorney gave a small, triumphant smile. "No further questions."

Landry left the stand, and Kowalski could see the strain on the sheriff's face. The man had done his duty, but the defence had managed to muddy the waters, just as they'd planned.

The Defence called the third witness, and a hush fell over the courtroom as the defendant's secretary, Jenny Caldwell, made her way to the front. She was a striking woman in her mid-thirties, wearing a figure-hugging dress that caught the attention of more than a few in the room.

"Miss Caldwell," he began, "how long have you been employed by Mr. Jacob?"

"About four years," she replied, her voice smooth and confident.

"And can you tell the court what your duties entail?"

Jenny smiled slightly, a practised expression. "I assist Mr. Jacob with the administrative side of his swamp tour business. I handle bookings, payments, and sometimes accompany him on tours."

The defence attorney nodded, setting the stage. "Now, on the night in question, can you tell us where Mr. Jacob was?"

"He was with me," Jenny answered without hesitation. "We were in bed together until about 3 AM. Then he got up, as he usually does, to check on the boats and make sure everything was ready for the first tour at 8 AM."

He raised an eyebrow. "And what time did Mr. Jacob return?"

"Around 6 AM," she said, her tone matter-of-fact.

"And during that time, did you notice anything unusual about his appearance? Any signs that he might have been involved in an altercation?"

Jenny shook her head. "No, nothing unusual. No blood, no torn clothes. He looked just as he always does."

The prosecutor nodded, sensing the jury's interest. "And you're certain of the time he left and returned?"

"Positive," she replied, her confidence unwavering.

The defence turned slightly, making eye contact with the jurors before asking his final question. "Miss Caldwell, in your time working for Mr. Jacob, have you ever known him to be violent?"

Jenny paused, glancing at Daryl Jacob, who gave her an almost imperceptible nod. "No, never," she finally said. "Daryl's always been kind and professional."

The defence gave a curt nod. "No further questions, Your Honor."

Travis was quick to his feet, he had one question: "From 3 am until 6 am, you cannot positively say where Daryl Jacobs was or what he was doing?"

Jenny hesitantly agreed, "No, not for definite."

"No further questions."

Jenny Caldwell walked back to her seat with the same poise she had displayed on the stand.

As the judge called for a recess, Kowalski watched the jurors file out, their expressions a mix of confusion and doubt. The first day of the trial had been a battle of narratives. Travis Hale had laid out the brutality of the crime, while the defence had begun to cast doubt on the idea that Daryl Jacob was the perpetrator.

But Kowalski wasn't done yet. He had seen enough trials to know that the tide could turn at any moment, and he had a few more cards to play. As he left the courtroom, blending into the crowd, he allowed himself a small smile. The game was just beginning.

CHAPTER TWENTY-EIGHT

The soft glow of the desk lamp did little to brighten the dim office. Shadows clung to the corners, where the light couldn't quite reach. Travis Hale sat behind his desk, staring at the crime scene photos splayed out in front of him. His hands were clasped tightly together, elbows on the desk, eyes narrowed with frustration. The day had been long, and nothing had gone as planned. He had been in the game long enough to know when the tide was against him, and today, the current had been nothing short of relentless.

Kowalski leaned back in a worn leather chair opposite Travis, rubbing his temples as if trying to stave off an oncoming headache. He hadn't seen his partner in a mood like this in a long time. Travis was usually the rock, the one who held it together when everything else was falling apart. But today, the cracks were starting to show.

"That was a disaster," Travis muttered, breaking the heavy silence. He didn't look up, his eyes still fixed on the photos, searching for something he knew wasn't there. "The evidence... it's too thin. We need that eyewitness tomorrow to tie Daryl Jacob to the scene."

Kowalski nodded slowly, the weight of the day settling into his bones. "He will."

Travis shook his head, finally looking up. The frustration in his eyes was unmistakable. "Not this time, Kowalski. I've got a bad feeling about this one. If we don't find something—anything—on him by tomorrow, he's going to walk. And you know what that means."

Kowalski didn't need him to spell it out. They'd both seen what happened when people like Daryl Jacob slipped through the cracks. He was too connected, too slick. If they didn't nail him now, they might never get another chance.

Before either of them could say anything more, a soft knock on the door broke the tension. It creaked open just a crack, and Mrs. Smith, Travis's trusted secretary, poked her head in.

"Evening, gentlemen," she said, stepping inside with a large brown paper bag and a thermos in hand. "Thought you might be hungry, so I took the liberty of ordering some Chinese takeout. And I brought you some of my special coffee." She placed the bag and thermos on the desk, giving them a reassuring smile.

Travis looked up at her, the tension in his face softening just a bit. "Thanks, Mrs. Smith. You didn't have to do that."

She waved a hand dismissively. "Nonsense. You two look like you haven't eaten all day, and I know how you get when you're stuck on a case." She turned to leave, then paused at the door. "I'm off home now, but don't stay too late. Tomorrow's another day."

"Goodnight, Mrs. Smith," Kowalski said, trying to muster up a smile for her sake.

"Goodnight, boys." She gave them one last look, her eyes full of the kind of understanding that only came with years of experience, and then she was gone.

For a moment, the room was quiet again, save for the faint hum of the city outside. Travis reached for the thermos, pouring the coffee into two chipped mugs that were permanently stationed on his desk. The smell of the rich brew filled the room, and for a moment, it seemed to take the edge off.

They ate in silence, both men lost in their own thoughts. The food was good, the coffee better, but it did little to lighten the mood. Travis knew what had to be done, but that didn't make it any easier.

When the last of the takeout was gone, and the coffee had cooled, Travis leaned back in his chair and fixed Kowalski with a serious look.

"Tomorrow," he said, his voice low but firm, "you've got to find me some dirt on Daryl Jacob. I don't care what it is—financials, old acquaintances, a speeding ticket—anything we can use to tie him down. If we don't, he's going to walk free, and then it's all on us."

Kowalski nodded, understanding the gravity of what Travis was saying. "I'll dig up everything I can. We'll find something."

"We better," Travis replied, his voice heavy with determination. "Because if we don't, this whole city's going to know we failed."

The silence that followed was thick with unspoken fears and the weight of responsibility that came with their job. Kowalski finished his coffee, the bitter taste lingering as he stood to leave.

"Get some rest, Travis," he said, though he knew it was unlikely his partner would heed the advice.

Travis didn't respond, his mind already elsewhere, turning over the problem again and again, searching for the answer that seemed just out of reach.

As Kowalski left the office, he couldn't shake the feeling that tomorrow was going to be even longer than today. But he also knew they had no choice. They had to stop Daryl Jacob, no matter what it took.

And for Travis Hale, failure was not an option.

CHAPTER TWENTY-NINE

The courtroom buzzed with a tense energy as day two of the trial commenced. The previous day's proceedings had been rocky, and the prosecution was scrambling to solidify its case against Daryl Jacob. Travis Hale sat at the prosecution table, his expression steely, eyes locked on the defendant. Today, they had to make some headway. They couldn't afford any more setbacks.

The judge called the court to order, and the next witness was summoned to the stand. An older man in his late fifties, with thinning hair and deep lines etched into his face, took the oath. His hands trembled slightly as he adjusted his glasses, but there was a resolve in his eyes that told everyone in the room he was ready to tell his story.

"Please state your name for the record," The Judge, said, her voice clear and steady.

"Earl Granger," the man replied, his voice a bit shaky at first but gaining strength as he spoke.

Travis Hale stood up, "Mr. Granger, can you tell the court where you were on the night of the incident?"

Earl nodded, shifting in his seat. "I was at home, in my trailer, at the park on the south side of town."

"And what did you witness that night?"

He took a deep breath, as if steeling himself for the memories that were about to flood back. "It was the middle of the night, around 4 AM, when I heard this crashing noise. It was loud enough to wake me up, and I don't usually wake up easy. I got out of bed and went to the window, and that's when I saw it. The trailer belonging to those two Black men—" he hesitated, searching for the right words, "—it was going up in flames."

A murmur ran through the courtroom, the gravity of his words sinking in. Travis nodded, urging him to continue.

"I saw them—saw those two men—jump out of the trailer, trying to get away from the fire. But before they could even catch their breath, a group of men came out of the shadows and started to beat them. I mean, really beat them. I watched in horror... didn't know what to do at first. Then I grabbed my phone and called the police."

Travis Hale leaned in slightly, his tone gentle but firm. "Mr. Granger, I understand this is difficult, but I need to ask you something very important. Did you see the defendant, Daryl Jacob, at the scene?"

Earl Granger's eyes flicked over to where Daryl Jacob sat, calm and composed, at the defence table. There was no hesitation in his voice now. "Yes. He was there. No doubt about it."

The courtroom fell silent as everyone processed this statement. It was the first real connection that had been made between Jacob and the crime.

Travis Hale let the silence hang for a moment before speaking again. "Thank you, Mr. Granger. No further questions."

The defence attorney was new today, a slick and seasoned man, Victor Baron was the best in the company, and when they wanted the case won and tied up quickly, he was sent for, he stood up and approached the witness stand with a predatory smile. He was known for his ruthless cross-examinations, and today would be no different.

"Mr. Granger," he began, his tone almost friendly, "thank you for your testimony. Now, we've established that you saw my client, Daryl Jacob, at the scene that night. But I need to ask you something crucial—did you see Mr. Jacob take part in the beating?"

Earl hesitated, the question hanging in the air like a guillotine blade. "Well... I assumed he did. He was with the group, and they all seemed to be in on it together."

Victor Barron pounced on the response. "So, you assumed he did. But, Mr. Granger, can you say for certain—without a shadow of a doubt—that you saw my client, Daryl Jacob, physically participate in the attack on those men?"

Earl opened his mouth, but the words seemed to stick in his throat. Finally, he shook his head. "No... I can't say for definite that he did."

The defence attorney's smile widened, the sharpness of it almost cutting. "So, in reality, Mr. Granger, you cannot definitively place my client as an active participant in the assault. All you can say is that he was there, correct?"

Earl Granger's shoulders slumped slightly, the weight of his answer pressing down on him. "Yes... that's correct."

"No further questions, Your Honor," Barron said, stepping back to his seat with a smug look of satisfaction. He knew he had just deflated a key point of the prosecution's case.

As Earl Granger was dismissed from the stand, Travis Hale clenched his jaw, frustration gnawing at him. Another setback. They had Daryl Jacob at the scene, but without clear evidence of his participation, it wasn't enough. The case was slipping through their fingers like sand, and the defence knew it.

As the Judge adjourned for the morning, Travis Hale's mind raced. They had to find something more—

something solid. Where was Kowalski? He hadn't called or answered, they needed a breakthrough, or Daryl Jacob would walk free, and justice would be left in the dust.

CHAPTER THIRTY

Kowalski's mind was a storm as he navigated the backroads of Houma, Louisiana. The day had started before dawn, fuelled by the mounting pressure from Travis Hale and the need to find something—anything—that could tie Daryl Jacob directly to the crime. The evidence so far was circumstantial, the witness testimony shaky at best. They needed more, and Kowalski was the man to get it.

The first place he hit was a dingy little bar on the outskirts of town called The Boxer and Barrel. It was the kind of place where the regulars were more familiar with the bottom of a bottle than they were with the world outside. The flickering neon sign out front buzzed like an angry wasp, casting an eerie glow over the cracked asphalt parking lot. Kowalski pushed open the creaky door and stepped inside, his eyes adjusting to the dim light.

The bartender, a wiry man in his fifties with a thick moustache and a perpetual scowl, eyed Kowalski with suspicion as he approached the bar.

"What can I get ya?" the bartender grunted, not bothering to hide his disinterest.

Kowalski pulled out his badge and a folded photo of Daryl Jacob, sliding it across the sticky counter. "I'm looking for information. Recognize this guy?"

The bartender's eyes flicked down to the photo, his scowl deepening as he studied it. He glanced back up at Kowalski, trying to gauge how much he could or should say.

"Yeah, I've seen him around," he said slowly, his voice low. "He comes in here from time to time. Usually keeps to himself, but he's got a crew he rolls with. They're not the friendly type, if you know what I mean."

"Do you remember seeing him a few nights ago?" Kowalski pressed, his tone growing more intense. "The night of the fire at the trailer park?"

The bartender nodded, more out of habit than cooperation. "Yeah, I remember. Him and a bunch of guys came in, had a few drinks, and then piled out into their trucks. Looked like they were on their way to do something they shouldn't be doing."

Kowalski's pulse quickened. This was the lead they needed. "How many men? Were they armed?"

"Hard to say," the bartender shrugged. "Maybe six or seven of 'em. As for being armed, they didn't exactly wave their guns around in here, but I wouldn't be surprised if they had some baseball bats in those trucks."

Kowalski thanked the bartender and left the bar, feeling a glimmer of hope for the first time that day. It wasn't solid evidence, but it was something—proof that Daryl Jacob was part of a group that could easily be connected to the violence at the trailer park.

But it wasn't enough. Not yet.

The next stop was one Kowalski dreaded, but he knew it had to be done. He drove across town to where—Juror 3—lived.

He parked his car a small distance away and walked the rest of the way, his heart pounding with unease. When he reached the house, a sleek black Doberman greeted him with a snarl, its lips curling back to reveal sharp teeth. The dog strained against the chain-link fence, growling menacingly as Kowalski approached.

"Easy, boy," Kowalski muttered, though the dog wasn't in the mood to listen. He kept his distance, pulling out the same photo of Daryl Jacob and holding it up for the man who had appeared on the porch, likely drawn by the dog's aggression.

The man was in his forties, with a shaved head and a build that spoke of regular workouts. He was dressed in a crisp polo shirt and khakis, but there was something about his eyes that made Kowalski's skin crawl—something cold, calculating.

"What do you want?" the man asked, his voice sharp.

Kowalski didn't mince words. "I'm Detective Kowalski, I need to know if you've seen this man around. Particularly at any...meetings."

The man's expression didn't change, but there was a flicker of recognition in his eyes as he glanced at the photo. "Meetings? What kind of meetings?"

Kowalski held his gaze, unflinching. "KKK meetings. Don't play dumb with me. We both know what goes on around here."

The man looked at the photo again, more closely this time. He took a moment, then gave a small nod, his expression hardening. "Yeah, I've seen him. Not often, but now and then. He's been at a few meetings, but he's not one of the regulars."

Kowalski felt a cold knot form in his stomach. It wasn't exactly what he wanted to hear, but it was enough to paint a clearer picture of Daryl Jacob—a picture that could be shown to the jury.

"Thanks," Kowalski said, tucking the photo back into his pocket. He turned to leave, but not before adding, "If you thought you were doing your duty by protecting him, you were wrong. He's going down for what he did."

He didn't wait for a response, and the man didn't offer one. The Doberman watched him go, still growling softly, as Kowalski made his way back to the car.

The sun was high in the bright blue afternoon sky. Kowalski drove back to Jacobs Swamp Tours; it was a hunch, but it might be the clincher.

But the clock was ticking, and he was running out of time.

Kowalski pulled up to Jacob's Swamp Tours, the sports Pontiac crunching over the gravel as he parked near the front. The place looked like it had been abandoned for years—windows boarded up, the paint on the sign peeling away, and not a soul in sight. The swamp tours had once been a thriving business, but now it was just another ghost in the bayou. The detective didn't waste any time; he knew he wouldn't find what he needed in the front. He made his way around to the back, where he found a cluttered repair yard and a dilapidated tool shop that looked like it hadn't been used in months. The lock on the door was rusted but not formidable, and with a hard shove, he forced his way inside.

The shop was a mess, with tools scattered across workbenches and piles of scrap metal littering the floor. Kowalski's heart pounded in his chest as he frantically searched through drawers and toolboxes, knowing he was running out of time. He almost missed it—a small metal box tucked away in a corner, half-hidden beneath a pile of greasy rags. He pried it open with trembling hands and froze. Inside, nestled among a set of old screwdrivers, was a knuckle duster. The metal was stained with what looked like dried blood, barely noticeable but unmistakable. Kowalski's breath caught in his throat. This could be the break they needed—the tangible evidence to link Daryl Jacob directly to the brutal beatings. He carefully pocketed the knuckle duster, his mind already racing with the implications.

Kowalski walked back to his car, his eyes scanning the dimming horizon as the unsettling feeling gnawed at him again. All day, he'd felt it someone was watching him. He couldn't shake the creeping sense of being followed, like shadows that clung too closely. As he reached for the door handle, something caught his attention a black SUV, half-hidden behind a cluster of Tupelo trees just out of sight, its dark windows glinting under the fading sun. Who was it? More of Daryl's rough crowd keeping tabs on him? Or maybe the defence team, nervous he'd uncover something that could blow their case wide open?

His mobile phone rang….

CHAPTER THIRTY-ONE

The courtroom sounded with the low hum of restless anticipation as the hands of the clock crept past one. Adjournment for lunch had come and gone, yet there was still no sign of Kowalski. The judge, a woman of stern demeanour and little patience, returned to her seat, the robe settling around her like a dark cloud as she brought the court back to order.

"Mr. Baron," the judge intoned, glancing over her half-moon glasses, "are you prepared to call your next witness?"

Victor Baron, the defence lawyer, rose with a deliberate calm. "Yes, Your Honor. The defence calls Ray Keller to the stand."

A murmur rippled through the room as Ray Keller was escorted to the witness stand. His presence was a stark contrast to the proceedings—muscular, tattooed, and with the rough-hewn look of a man who had seen more than his share of life's darker corners. Already convicted of grievous bodily harm against two men, as well as arson, Keller's reputation preceded him.

Travis Hale, the prosecutor, had already voiced his objections earlier in the day. He had fought to keep Keller off the stand, arguing vehemently that his association with the defendant, Daryl Jacob, tainted any testimony he might give. But the judge had overruled him, allowing Keller's words to be heard.

Baron approached the witness with an air of casual confidence, as if the entire outcome of this trial didn't hinge on what was about to unfold.

"Mr. Keller," Baron began, his voice measured and calm, "was my client, Daryl Jacob, present at the scene of the crime on the night in question?"

"Yes," Keller replied, his voice a gravelly monotone, the single word hanging in the air like a weight.

"And was he involved in the violent assault on the two men?" Baron's tone was unyielding, but there was a softness in his eyes, as if he were coaxing the truth from the depths of Keller's memory.

"No," Keller said, shaking his head slightly. "In fact, he was there to try and stop us."

The statement landed like a hammer blow in the courtroom. A collective gasp, barely audible, seemed to suck the air from the room. Travis Hale, sitting rigid behind his table, shook his head in disbelief, his face a mask of frustration and disbelief. The delicate threads of his carefully woven case were unravelling before his eyes, each word from Keller pulling at the seams.

Hale didn't even bother to cross-examine. There was no point. He could see the jury's expressions shifting, the weight of Keller's words sinking in. A master of the courtroom, Hale knew when the tide had turned against him, and this was one of those moments.

The judge, sensing the shift in the air, leaned forward. "Mr. Hale, are you ready for closing arguments?"

Hale straightened his tie, clearing his throat to buy a moment's time. "Your Honor, I request a brief recess—ten minutes—to make a phone call."

The judge considered this for a moment, then nodded. "Very well, Mr. Hale. You have ten minutes. The court is in recess."

The gavel struck wood, and the tension in the room briefly dissipated as people began to stir. Hale, however, was already moving with purpose, his mind racing as he headed for the exit. He needed to regroup, to find a way to salvage his case in these final moments. The stakes were too high to let this slip away now. He called Kowalski one last time.

Victor Baron remained seated; his expression impassive as he watched Hale's retreating figure. He knew the prosecution was in trouble, and it wasn't a position Hale was accustomed to. The next ten minutes would be crucial, but Baron wasn't worried. The truth, it seemed, had a way of revealing itself, no matter how deeply it had been buried.

As the courtroom emptied for the brief recess, Baron allowed himself a small, private smile. The defence had played its card, and now all they had to do was wait for the final act to unfold.

CHAPTER THIRTY-TWO

Travis Hale burst out of the courtroom; the heavy door swinging shut behind him with a muted thud. His heart pounded in his chest, and his mind raced as he fumbled for his phone. The prosecution's case was hanging by a thread, and he knew it. He had only one option left—a desperate one, but it was the only play he had.

He dialled Kowalski's number with trembling fingers, silently willing his investigator to pick up. "Come on, come on," he muttered under his breath, pacing the hallway. Each ring seemed to last an eternity.

Finally, there was a click. "Boss," Kowalski's voice crackled on the other end, gruff and hurried.

"Kowalski, where the hell are you?" Travis demanded, his voice low and tense. "We're on closing arguments. We need you here now!"

"I'm on my way," Kowalski replied, the sound of an engine revving in the background. "I've got two witnesses. One who saw Daryl with that group of guys in a bar, heading off together. The other saw him at a KKK meeting, and at his workshop, I found a knuckle duster with a hint of blood on it. Boss, this is the smoking gun we needed."

Travis felt a surge of adrenaline. "Good. Damn good. But I need more time. Get here as fast as you can. I'll do what I can to delay the trial until you arrive."

Kowalski's voice was grim but determined. "I'm pushing it, boss. You've got to buy me an hour, tops."

"I'll handle it," Travis said, ending the call with a swift tap. He took a deep breath, steadying himself. The stakes had never been higher. Without this evidence, his case would crumble. With it, he might just secure the conviction he was after.

Travis stormed back into the courtroom, his face a mask of controlled urgency. The judge, who had just resumed her seat, raised an eyebrow at the prosecutor's abrupt entrance. The room fell silent, every eye on Hale as he approached the bench.

"Your Honor," Travis began, his voice carrying a newfound intensity, "I have just received word that we have new evidence and two crucial witnesses who can provide testimony that directly implicates the defendant, Daryl Jacob, in the crimes we are prosecuting. I respectfully request a delay until tomorrow to present this evidence."

Victor Baron, the defence lawyer, was on his feet in an instant, his objection sharp and cutting. "Your Honor, this is an unacceptable delay. The prosecution has had ample time to present their case. The defence vehemently opposes any postponement. This is nothing more than a desperate attempt to salvage a case that is falling apart."

The judge, a seasoned figure of authority, leaned back in her chair, her gaze shifting from Hale to Baron and then back again. The tension in the room was palpable. She tapped her fingers thoughtfully on the bench, the rhythmic sound echoing in the stillness.

"Mr. Hale," the judge said slowly, weighing her words, "this is highly irregular. However, I understand the gravity of the situation. If your man is back here within the hour, I will consider your request. But let me be clear—if he is not here, we will proceed with closing arguments as scheduled. Do you understand?"

Travis nodded, the weight of the judge's words sinking in. "Yes, Your Honor. Thank you."

The judge's gavel struck wood, signalling another brief recess. Travis hurried out of the courtroom, his mind a whirlwind of strategy and uncertainty. He had one hour—sixty minutes to keep his case from unravelling completely.

As the minutes ticked by, Travis could only hope that Kwalski would make it in time. The courtroom, once again hushed in anticipation, felt like a pressure cooker about to explode. Both sides of the room were on edge, aware that the fate of the trial hung in the balance.

Travis Hale knew that this was his last chance, his final gambit in a case that had already taken so many unexpected turns. All he could do now was wait—and pray that Kowalski's arrival would be the key to turning the tide in his favour.

CHAPTER THIRTY-THREE

Kowalski burst into the courtroom, the sudden crash of the doors startling everyone in the room. The clatter of papers and the low murmur of conversation halted abruptly as all eyes turned toward him. The judge's gavel struck the bench once, sharply, but there was more curiosity than reprimand in her tone as she looked down from the bench.

"Kowalski, you seem to have something urgent," Judge Mansfield said, her voice measured, though her eyes betrayed a hint of irritation.

Victor Baron, the defence attorney, exchanged a wary glance with Prosecutor Travis Hale. Both men stood, neither sure what to expect from Kowalski's dramatic entrance. The judge, with a sigh that spoke of many years of dealing with unexpected chaos, gestured for all three to follow her to her chambers.

"Let's handle this privately," the judge said, standing and leading them out of the courtroom.

In the quiet of the judge's chambers, the tension hung thick. Mansfield took her seat behind the large oak desk, eyes shifting between Kowalski, Baron, and Hale.

"Alright," the judge said, folding her hands. "What's this about, Kowalski? You've interrupted proceedings. I hope you have something worth the spectacle."

Kowalski stood tall, his breath heavy from both the rush to get there and the weight of what he was about to reveal. He pulled a small notebook from his pocket, flipping through the pages before speaking.

"I've got new evidence," Kowalski said, locking eyes with Judge Mansfield. "The bartender at the pub where the group of men met before the attack—he's identified Daryl. He saw Daryl in the bar that night, mingling with the same men who left to carry out the assault. This connects him directly to the perpetrators."

The judge frowned, leaning back in her chair. "It's already been established that Daryl was at the scene of the attack, Kowalski. He never disputed that. This is redundant information and adds nothing new to the case. I'm afraid this is inadmissible."

Kowalski's lips tightened, but he pressed on, flipping to another page in his notebook. "There's testimony from a witness stating that Daryl attended KKK meetings, which could establish a pattern of behaviour and motive."

Victor Baron scoffed from his side of the room, but the judge spoke before he could interject. "And who is this witness?" Judge Mansfield asked.

"Juror 3," Kowalski answered.

A palpable silence filled the room before the judge shook her head. "Juror 3? Kowalski, you've already discarded him as biassed during jury selection. His testimony is unreliable and inadmissible in this case."

Frustration flashed across Kowalski's face, but he wasn't finished. "There's more. We found something. At Daryl's Swamp Tours property, we discovered a knuckle duster with dried blood on it, hard evidence that ties him directly to the attack."

The judge leaned forward slightly, as if considering it, but Baron was quick to respond. "And was this obtained legally, Kowalski?" Baron's voice dripped with confidence, already knowing the answer.

Kowalski paused for just a moment too long. "No... it wasn't. We didn't have a warrant, but—"

"Then it's inadmissible," Judge Mansfield cut him off, her voice final. He rubbed his temples, clearly exhausted by the legal back-and-forth. "You know better than this. If the evidence wasn't obtained with a warrant, it's not entering this courtroom."

Kowalski's shoulders sagged slightly. Every path he had hoped to pursue had just been blocked by procedure, by law, by the very system he had sworn to protect. He looked to Hale, hoping for some backup, but the prosecutor's expression was grim, understanding that they'd come up empty.

"I'm sorry, Kowalski," the judge said, her voice softer now. "I appreciate your dedication, but this isn't going anywhere. We need to return to the courtroom for closing arguments."

Kowalski stood in silence as the judge rose, and the others followed suit. His mind raced, searching for some last-ditch option, some way to get the truth in front of the jury, but it was clear there would be no miracle today.

As they filed back toward the courtroom, the weight of failure sat heavy on Kowalski's chest. This wasn't how he had imagined it going. The evidence, the connections he had been so sure. But now, all he could do was watch as the case ended without the revelations he had hoped to bring.

The door to the courtroom swung open, and they re-entered the space where the jury waited. Closing arguments were all that was left now.

CHAPTER THIRTY-FOUR

The courtroom was tense as Victor Baron, the defence attorney, wrapped up his closing argument with the smooth confidence of a man who knew he had done his job. He paced slowly before the jury, his voice calm, almost paternal.

"Ladies and gentlemen, what the prosecution has presented to you is a collection of assumptions, not proof. Yes, my client, Daryl Jacob, was at the scene, but there is no solid evidence that links him to the crime they accuse him of. They want you to believe he's guilty by association—because of who he knows, where he was. But that is not how justice works in this country. You cannot convict a man without evidence. And they've given you none. I trust that you will see that the prosecution's case falls apart on close inspection and deliver the only verdict that makes sense."

With a final, confident nod, Baron returned to his seat, looking satisfied. Daryl, sitting beside him, stared straight ahead, unflinching, his expression a mask of calm. He didn't look at the jury, but Kowalski could see the hint of arrogance in the way his hands rested calmly on the table. He was waiting for this to be over.

Prosecutor Travis Hale stood next, his eyes sharp, his jaw tight as he faced the jury for the last time. He knew he had an uphill battle, especially after the judge had thrown out the crucial pieces of evidence Kowalski had rushed in with. But he was determined.

"Ladies and gentlemen," Hale began, his voice firm, "I ask you not to be distracted by smoke and mirrors. The defence wants you to forget the context, forget the brutality of the attack on two innocent men. They want you to ignore the fact that Daryl Jacob was with the very group responsible. You've seen enough to know he played a role in orchestrating what happened that night. The evidence may not be wrapped in a bow, but it's there if you look closely. A 'not guilty' verdict would send the message that Daryl Jacob and others like him can commit acts of violence and hide behind the shadows of reasonable doubt. I ask you to see the truth and find Daryl Jacob guilty."

Hale stepped back, his words hanging in the air as the judge gave her final instructions to the jury before sending them to deliberate. Kowalski watched them file out, each face giving little away. They had listened intently, but would they see through the web of legal technicalities? Or would Daryl Jacob Walk free?

As the hours passed, the courtroom was a storm of silence. Kowalski sat back in his chair, his mind churning. He couldn't shake the feeling that the system had failed. Everything pointed to Daryl being involved—

maybe even being the mastermind—but without the admissible evidence to back it up, what could they do?

Two hours later, the jury returned, their faces set with a decision that no one could read. Hale's stomach tightened as the foreman handed the piece of paper to the judge.

Judge Mansfield unfolded the paper and read the verdict aloud, her voice steady. "On the charge of attempted murder in the first degree, how do you find the defendant?"

The room held its breath.

"Not guilty."

A murmur swept through the courtroom, followed by the judge's voice again.

"On the charge of attempted murder in the second degree, how do you find the defendant?"

"Not guilty."

The words seemed to hang in the air, heavy with finality. A wave of relief washed over Victor Baron and Daryl Jacob. Baron allowed himself a small, victorious smile, while Daryl sat motionless, only the slightest curl at the corner of his mouth betraying his satisfaction.

Travis Hale felt a sickening pit in his stomach. It was over. Daryl was walking out of here free, untouched, as if the violence and bloodshed were nothing more than a forgotten chapter in someone else's life.

The judge thanked the jury, dismissed them, and brought down the gavel, officially closing the case. The gallery began to clear out slowly, a buzz of conversation filling the room, but Kowalski stayed seated, his fists clenched. Travis Hale stood beside him, his face grim, staring straight ahead as if trying to process the loss.

As Daryl Jacob rose from his seat, he moved with an easy, deliberate grace, heading toward the door. Before he left, though, he paused just long enough to catch Kowalski's eye. A smirk played across Daryl's lips, the kind of smile that carried the weight of knowing he'd beaten the system. And then, in full view of the court, he lifted his hand, flipped his middle finger toward Kowalski and Hale, and left the room.

It was a taunt, a final act of defiance, and it stung. Kowalski's teeth ground together as he watched Daryl saunter out, a free man. Hale muttered something under his breath, too low to hear, but his posture reflected the same bitter disappointment that Kowalski felt.

Kowalski stood slowly, his mind already shifting. They had lost this battle, but the war wasn't over. Daryl might be walking free today, but who knows what will happen tomorrow....

CHAPTER THIRTY-FIVE

Daryl Jacob rose early, as he always did, in the quiet hours before dawn. The swamp was still, the thick, humid air clinging to everything like a second skin. He relished the solitude, the way the world felt empty before the tourists started arriving. Business had been slow after the trial, but slowly, people were starting to return. They always did. It didn't take long for memories to fade, and soon enough, his swamp tours would be booming again. He leaned over the side of his boat, checking the rigging, the engine, everything in place for the day ahead. The full moon hung high in the sky, casting a silver glow over the murky water, but Daryl's mind was focused elsewhere.

As he worked, unseen in the shadows, someone waited. A figure, hidden by the darkness, crept closer. The blade of the sword glinted in the moonlight as he advanced slowly, methodically, moving with the silence of a predator stalking its prey. He kept to the shadows, careful to avoid any noise that might alert Daryl. His eyes locked onto his target—Daryl's back was turned, oblivious, too focused on his tasks to notice the danger approaching.

The figure's heart pounded in his chest, each step calculated, deliberate. The sword was steady in his hand, the cold steel reflecting the eerie moonlight. Closer now, just a few more steps. He raised the blade, preparing for the swift strike that would end it all. One clean swipe across the neck, and Daryl Jacob would be gone, justice delivered in silence.

Suddenly, a voice shattered the stillness. "Freeze! Or I'll shoot!"

The figure spun around, sword still raised, his breath catching in his throat. Two guns were trained on him, both gleaming under the moonlight. Romano stood firm, his gun unwavering, while Rodriguez moved in from the other side, equally ready to fire. They had been watching him, trailing him, waiting for him to make his move. There was no escape.

"Drop the weapon," Romano barked, his voice cold and authoritative. "Now!"

For a brief second, the figure's grip on the sword tightened, eyes darting between the two detectives. Daryl, hearing the commotion, whipped around, his eyes wide with panic. The realization hit him in waves—how close he had come to death. He scrambled back, nearly tripping over the side of the boat as he fled toward safety.

The would-be attacker—Kowalski—stood frozen, the weight of his decision crashing down on him. Slowly, his hands trembled, and the sword slipped from his grasp, falling to the ground with a dull thud. He didn't look at Daryl. His eyes remained fixed on the gun barrels pointed at him.

Rodriguez moved in quickly, securing Kowalski's wrists with a set of handcuffs, his face a mix of disappointment and resignation. Kowalski didn't resist. He stood motionless as the cold metal bit into his skin.

"Guess you thought no one was watching," Rodriguez muttered as she locked the cuffs tight.

Kowalski said nothing, his gaze distant, fixed on the moonlit swamp beyond the boat. It was supposed to have been over quickly, and cleanly. His frustration with the justice system, with Daryl walking free after the trial, had driven him to this. But now, standing in the quiet of the swamp, with Romano and Rodriguez leading him away, he realised the depths of his mistake.

As Romano holstered his gun, he gave Kowalski a hard look. "You have thrown your life away tonight. And for what? He's not worth it."

Kowalski didn't answer. He let himself be led away, the swamp slowly swallowing the silence again as Daryl, still shaken, leaned against his boat. The night had almost claimed him, but somehow, fate or justice had intervened.

EPILOGUE

Travis Hale sat alone in his dimly lit office, the muted glow of the desk lamp casting long shadows across the walls. The office, once a bustling hub of legal power, now felt like a tomb of forgotten victories. The framed commendations and accolades, once symbols of his success, now served only as reminders of a time long past. The leather chair behind his desk had long lost its shine, and the pile of case files stacked haphazardly on the corner of his desk seemed to grow taller by the day.

The only companion Hale had were these evenings was a half-empty bottle of Jack Daniels. He stared at it with a mix of resignation and hope, the amber liquid reflecting his own tarnished ambitions. It had become a ritual: pour a drink, take a long, contemplative sip, and stare out the window at the city that once looked up to him. The city that now felt so indifferent.

Mrs. Smith, his loyal paralegal and the keeper of his once-great reputation, had retired last year. She had taken leave to care for her husband, who was battling Alzheimer's. Hale had been happy for her, though he couldn't deny that her departure had left him with a gnawing sense of emptiness. She had been the last link to the glory days, and without her, the office felt like a hollow echo of its former self.

Kowalski, a name that once reverberated through courtrooms and news headlines, was now a distant memory. Five life sentences and one attempted murder—Kowalski was a symbol of everything Hale had once been able to achieve. Now, he sat in a small, sterile cell, waiting for his end.

The daily grind of petty thefts, domestic abuse cases, and DUI charges were a far cry from the high-stakes dramas that once defined his career. He handled them with the same meticulous care, but the thrill was gone. Each case felt like a drop in a vast ocean of mediocrity. The victories were small, the challenges minor. It was a far cry from the complex legal battles and high-profile cases that had once been his domain.

As the evening wore on, Hale poured another glass of Jack Daniels, the rich, smoky flavour a comfort against the backdrop of his diminishing career. He leaned back in his chair, allowing the warmth of the whisky to seep through him. His mind wandered to the future—he was waiting for the case that would pull him out of this rut. The big case. The one that would put him back in the spotlight, restore his reputation, and remind everyone of why he had once been the go-to prosecutor.

He glanced at the clock on the wall, its hands ticking steadily toward midnight. The phone on his desk was silent, the absence of its ring a constant reminder of his status. He knew that at any moment, a case might walk through that door, a case that would be his chance to reclaim his former glory. Until then, he would wait and drink, clinging to the hope that his name would once again be associated with the high-profile victories that had defined his career.

Hale took another sip, letting the alcohol burn a path down his throat, and stared at the ceiling, lost in thought. The city outside was a sprawling labyrinth of opportunity and neglect, and he was waiting for that one chance to navigate it once more. Until then, he was content to keep company with the bottle and the fading echoes of his past triumphs, hoping that someday, the phone would ring and bring him the case that would lift him back to the big time. In the meantime, he had to prosecute a Mr Knight, accused of sexually abusing his daughter.

Printed in Great Britain
by Amazon